A HUGS-AND-KISSES FAMILY

BY
MEREDITH WEBBER

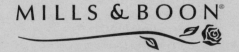

MILLS & BOON®

First published in Great Britain 1999
Harlequin Mills & Boon Limited,
Eton House, 18-24 Paradise Road, Richmond, Surrey TW9 1SR

© Meredith Webber 1999

ISBN 0 263 81817 9

Set in Times Roman 10½ on 12 pt.
03-9910-51316-D

Printed and bound in Spain
by Litografia Rosés S.A., Barcelona

PROLOGUE

'So, WHAT are your plans when you return to Australia?'
Alain asked.

Angus studied his new friend as he considered the
question—considered the merits of answering truthfully.
Alain Corot had been his lifeline to the real world during
his seven weeks' incarceration in hospital, his host for
another frustrating fortnight of convalescence before doctors deemed him well enough to return home.

Now, as they sat in the lounge of Charles De Gaulle
airport, waiting on the boarding call for Angus's flight
home, he knew the friendship was an ephemeral thing,
unlikely to progress beyond reciprocal Christmas cards.

Which might make Alain the perfect confidant!
Someone on whom Angus could test his thoughts aloud
and gauge their truth for his own assurance.

'I am going to woo and win back my ex-wife,' he
answered, hoping he sounded more positive than he felt.
'I intend to lay siege to her, to prove my love, and, most
importantly, get us both back on the IVF programme until
she conceives the child she wants so badly.'

There. It was out. The bald summation of the thoughts
which had churned and tangled in his head since his re-
patriation to France—or since he'd become aware enough
of his surroundings and sufficiently conscious to link
words together in his head.

'She is beautiful, this ex-wife?'

Angus grinned. He knew Alain well enough to guess
his analysis of female charms was a cover for an innate

5

shyness. In the time Angus had known him, Alain had looked, but hadn't touched.

'Darkly beautiful—like that painting of the Madonna we saw in that special display of Murillo's paintings at the Louvre.'

'The *Virgin and Child*? I thought you lingered over-long before it. That is why you wish to make her pregnant? Because the painting appealed to you?'

'The painting did appeal to me—but as a magnificent work of art, not a reason for conceiving a child,' Angus explained. He hesitated but, having come this far in what was, to all intents and purposes, a confession, he decided to continue.

'Jenessa, my wife, wanted a child very badly. Not at first, as we married while we were both studying, but after five years of marriage we decided to stop taking precautions—well, we decided she should stop taking the Pill which was the only form of contraception we'd ever practised.'

'And you were happy about this? It was a joint decision?'

Alain had tilted his body forward in his chair, his physical language suggesting an interest which made it easier for Angus to continue.

'Happy enough.' Angus shrugged away the discomfort of the small lie, then realised that if he was to commit himself to a future with Jenessa, he had to begin with the truth.

'I was ambivalent,' he admitted. 'I was a loner, always had been, from the time of my parents' divorce when I was parcelled off to live with my father—he got the boy, my mother the girl. Finding Jenessa, it was like finding a soul-mate—the other half of myself. I suppose, if I'm honest, I was afraid a child would not so much come between us but dilute our closeness.'

'And as the child of divorced parents, you, no doubt, felt yourself in part to blame for their problems. That's a well-documented scenario.'

Angus acknowledged the comment with a nod. Being separated from his sister, that had, at the time, increased his feelings of somehow being the cause of the trouble; living with his father, that had been his punishment for sins he'd been unaware of committing.

'You said "back on the IVF programme",' Alain prompted. 'She had trouble conceiving? You have already plunged your toes into those waters?'

'Have we ever? And don't let anyone tell you it's easy. It's not so much the tests but the highs of hope and deep troughs of disappointment when another strategy has failed. I went along with it for a year then baulked and said no more. I was honest with Jen about my feelings—'

'You *told* her you didn't want a child?' Alain's voice rose in disbelief, his slight accent becoming stronger with his emotional reaction.

Again Angus shrugged, remembering their third partner in the practice, Jack Nielsen, reacting in exactly the same way.

'It seemed best to tell the truth,' he muttered. 'I had this silly idea she might be going through all the rigmarole for my sake; that she might feel guilty about not producing "our" child.'

He used the hand gesture he hated to put the word in inverted commas, anxious Alain should understand his feelings at the time. Not that he'd understood them himself, not fully. Back then, he'd believed that once they'd got off the programme it would mean an automatic return to their pre-IVF life. He'd imagined the strain between himself and Jenessa would miraculously vanish, the forced aspect of their sex life, programmed and controlled by temperatures and fertility drugs, would disappear, and love would reign supreme.

'And was she?' Alain zeroed in on the problem.

'No. Well, not entirely. I think she did feel an inadequacy.' He hesitated, wondering how far to take this confession stuff. Deleted the next bit and continued, 'But she genuinely wanted a child. She'd also had a lonely childhood. I suppose it's what drew us together, made our bonds so much stronger. What I hadn't realised was that she'd had this vision of a family from the time she was a young girl. It had been a dream she'd clung to when times were bad.'

'Which made her failure to conceive so much harder for her to accept,' Alain suggested. 'Yet it is strange she didn't share this dream with you—before marriage, or certainly earlier in it.'

Angus felt the burden of responsibility swell like a huge tumour in his chest.

Truth time, he reminded himself.

'Oh, she shared it—if by sharing you mean telling me from time to time, talking about it at odd moments when we were happy with each other and relatively relaxed. But you know what medicine is like, Alain. Having two doctors in one family, that simply doubles the lack of time you have for close communication. During our early intern years we were lucky to see each other once a day, to spend a night together once a week. And when we were together there were more important things to worry about than the future—like sex, and working out our schedules so we knew when we might have it again.'

Alain chuckled.

'This is your perception of those early years, or hers also?'

'Good question! It's definitely mine. I remember being obsessed by it—not so much the sex, but the organisation it took to arrange it. I kept thinking, But I'm married, it shouldn't have to be this way! I guess Jen may have seen it differently although at the time she seemed as frantically caught up in our strategies as I was.'

'But internship doesn't go on for ever,' Alain pointed out. 'You were in private practice, before volunteering for Africa. Admittedly a practice can be busy but not so demanding, so frenetic.'

Angus stared across the terminal building to where tall windows allowed him a glimpse of a pale blue sky. He smiled then answered, 'No, it didn't last for ever. In fact, as we settled into a more regular life, I couldn't think why the sex had been so important. Marriage—the togetherness, the sharing of ideas and ideals, working together with a joint purpose—all became very special, Jenessa extraordinarily dear to me, our life complete, perfect. Or so I thought.'

Alain was silent for a moment, then he asked, with a tentative smile, 'Until she began to talk of having a baby?'

The intercom announced the boarding call for several planes and Angus pretended to be listening to the French words while he contemplated a reply. Having gone this far with Alain, he wanted to complete the explanation, particularly as the next person likely to confront him with questions would be Jenessa. Yet the words 'Singapore' and 'Sydney' had been clear enough. It was his flight they were calling.

He thanked Alain for his help and company, promised to keep in touch and said goodbye, but his friend's question remained with him, likely to be an unwanted and intrusive companion on the long flight ahead.

As he shook Alain's hand he thrust the thought aside, reminding himself of his goal.

'I will woo and win Jenessa,' he whispered to himself as he walked down the tunnel to board the plane, the words becoming a mantra to be repeated over and over again until they became a certainty in his mind.

CHAPTER ONE

THE final leg of the journey, a domestic flight from Sydney, seemed to take forever but finally the plane dropped lower, crossing the dense green of the Border Ranges into Queensland, then sweeping out over an indigo sea, losing altitude on the approach to Coolangatta Airport. Angus blinked back the unexpected moisture in his eyes. It was tiredness from the flight, undertaken too soon after his release from hospital. Anyone would feel emotional, coming home after such an ordeal.

Coming home?

Did he have a home?

His mood swung so dramatically he moved his shoulder experimentally. Definite discomfort, a slight throbbing, but not bad enough to be making him feel gloomy and depressed.

Gloomy and depressed? Where had those emotions sprung from? He'd been buoyed by images of this moment of touchdown since he'd left Paris about a century ago. Keyed up and excited at the thought of returning home—yes, of course, he had a home. It was right there in the suburb of Palm Beach, in the city of the Gold Coast, Queensland, the World, the Universe!

He remembered writing just such an elaborate address on his notebooks at school many years ago, and, now he considered it, he felt about as much insecurity right now as he had back then.

The plane taxied towards the terminal, the small buildings growing larger as the distance decreased, the activity on the tarmac increasing, while his mind skittered about, talking to itself, arguing and reassuring—totally confused.

OK, so, ethically, the house on the beach was no longer his home. He'd told Jenessa to keep it when he'd taken off for Africa, said they'd sort out finances some time in the future, but in the meantime she should stay on there, close to her work in a practice attached to John Flynn Hospital.

Legally, he still owned half of it as their divorce hadn't included a settlement. They'd hurried through the paperwork, with a minimum separation that was more in theory than in fact as he'd stayed on in the spare room of the house until he'd left. In fact, a divorce had been the last thing on his mind, although he'd been the first to admit their marriage had broken down and to make plans which hadn't included Jenessa. It was she who'd insisted they make it official, determined he should be free before he went away.

But freedom was a nebulous concept. Not like a suitcase you could pack and carry with you. Like 'home', it was more a state of mind.

The plane had slowed, stopped. He burrowed back into his seat and watched other passengers stand up, stretch, reach for baggage in the overhead compartments, chattering excitedly like kids released from school.

He'd wait until the end of the queue rather than be jostled, then he'd walk across to a phone booth and call Jen, warn her he was back so she didn't have a heart attack when she arrived home from work and found the place occupied.

In a day or two, maybe a week, once he'd seen the specialists and knew what was what, he'd find some other accommodation. Surely that would be better for his plan than staying in the house. After all, wooing included phone calls, arriving on her doorstep with bunches of flowers. Would it work if they were living together?

Air filled his lungs and he released it in a heartfelt sigh. It had all seemed easier when he'd been in Paris.

In the meantime, he was reasonably certain she wouldn't mind him returning to the spare room. After all, they'd been friends before they'd become lovers, had remained friends right through their marriage although even friendship had become a bit strained as the dreary process of IVF had begun, and the failures had become hard to accept. Yet, in all their cool pre-divorce discussions, they'd assured themselves the friendship would remain for ever; that, by divorcing, they would preserve it, perhaps make it stronger.

He struggled to his feet, aware of the sudden emptiness around him. Well, emptiness was nothing new. It had dwelt within him for a long time now—where freedom should be, he supposed.

'Do you need a hand?'

The blonde hostess was eyeing him a trifle warily. He'd exchanged small talk with her earlier when he'd asked for water to take a painkiller. Did she think he'd stayed behind to ask her for a date?

'No, I'm fine. I sat back to let the crowd go first. I've only got this carry-on bag so won't have to queue for baggage.'

She smiled and stood aside to let him pass her in the narrow aisle between the seats.

'Enjoy your stay,' she said, and sounded as if she meant it.

'I hope so,' he replied, recognising his reluctance to disembark for what it was. Fear that Jenessa might not be quite as delighted by his return as he was. Might not want to be wooed and won.

Of course she would be! Well, at least she'd be pleased about his return even if she wasn't in a wooing frame of mind.

Jenessa, he reminded himself, would always welcome him. It was her nature to be welcoming, as well as being sensible, practical and in control.

OK, so maybe not about everything. Her determination to become pregnant, the months of tests and treatment, of humiliating visits to specialists, time spent in small cubicles producing sperm while probes drew eggs from Jen's drug-swollen ovaries, had shown him a side of Jen he hadn't realised existed.

His feet hit the tarmac and he sighed, then shook his head and smiled, remembering not the increasingly tense and distancing time when every month had seemed like a mountain, climbed with hope before plunging into a bottomless abyss of despair. No, he was remembering his last night in Australia, when they'd celebrated their divorce, celebrated it as they had their marriage, with dinner at the Sheraton, too much wine and a night of unbridled lust.

He'd been surprised—and delighted—to rediscover their compatibility in bed. Lovemaking had died in the doomed process of baby-making. First it had turned into sex, rigidly controlled by temperatures and blood tests, then later even sex had been avoided lest it interrupt the chemical processes being undertaken to achieve pregnancy. In the end, they'd shared the big bed as strangers, and eventually he'd moved into the spare bedroom, more comfortable in his own space.

He entered the terminal building, moving swiftly through the jostling crowds towards a vacant phone-booth. Lifted the receiver, pushed coins into the slot, and dialled the surgery through the hospital switchboard so he'd speak to Jen first, not whoever was on reception duties.

'Dr Blair, please. It's Dr McLeod calling.'

Saying their two names, it produced a grim smile as he waited. When things had been bad between them he'd accused her of wanting a child more than marriage, using her refusal to change her professional name as a weapon, although he'd agreed with her reasoning at the time of her decision.

'Angus? Is that you? I can't believe it. How are you? Where are you? I didn't think you'd ever get to a phone to call me. Did you get the letter? Do you mind very much?'

The words rushed together, barely registering as his heart did a soft-shoe shuffle in response to her familiar, husky voice.

It's the normal reaction of any traveller, he told himself, and tried to make his tongue work properly, his mind form a rational sentence.

'I'm not in Africa. I'm home. Coolangatta Airport. Rang to see if you could put me up for the night or two.'

How pathetic! He sounded like a supplicant!

'You're home!' The words were a wail of—what? Despair?

'Oh, Angus, you didn't have to come home. I'd have managed, am managing, and I know it was the very last thing you wanted. Of course you can stay. I'm sorry I can't get away right now, but I'll be home later. Or in the morning. I'm running a sleep clinic over at the hospital this weekend but I should be able to get away for a while at least. Oh Angus, I'm—'

He was cut off, but not before he'd realised she was

crying. No, he must be wrong. Jenessa never cried. Not even when he'd wanted to howl his frustration to the moon, seeing her despair, feeling her anguish, at yet another unsuccessful IVF attempt. She'd walked around the house dry-eyed. At work she'd smiled and acted as if nothing had happened so only he had seen the gradual retreat of the laughing positive woman he'd married and watched the silent remote shadow of that person take her place.

He left the terminal building, his mind replaying the disjointed sentences he'd managed to retain. 'Didn't have to come home'? 'The very last thing you wanted'?

Oh, hell! She was involved with someone else. Was she living with the fellow? Him with her?

His mantra clanged loudly in his ears, followed by derisive, hollow laughter as his uncertain self mocked his naïvety.

He climbed into the cab, gave the address, agreed that the weather looked great and felt his stomach heave, then settle, as anger overwhelmed the shock of that initial realisation. All the pleasant 'let's be friends' stuff, the generous 'you have the house' declaration, was forgotten as a wave of black jealousy swept over him.

The bastard had better not be living with her—not in *his* house!

'This the place? Great spot, right here on the beach. Not many of the old cottages left. You done this one up inside?'

The taxi driver was being polite, but Angus couldn't marshal the manners necessary to reply. He dug through his limited luggage to find the bunch of keys someone had been sensible enough to pack for him when he'd been airlifted out of Africa. Now he clutched them in his hand like a weapon as he thrust a note at the driver and said, 'Keep the change.' He clambered out of the cab, striding towards the door before the man had started his engine.

Must be the wrong key. Tried another.

No luck.

Damn the woman—had she changed the locks? Had 'he', whoever he might be, had them changed in some pretence at ownership? Damn him and damn Jenessa! Spoiling his return like this. Moving the goalposts.

He'd see about that—move them back again if necessary. She was his—as he was hers. Hadn't their final night together proven as much?

He jammed another key into the lock and wriggled it about, his mind chasing along its own lines.

At first, when he'd been told he couldn't return to Africa, he'd been devastated, his dream of a lengthy stint of service to others defeated by a drug-addicted kid and an organism so small it could barely be seen under intense magnification.

Then he'd begun to see it as a master-stroke of fate— a once-in-a-lifetime second chance. The notion of winning and wooing Jen had beckoned to him like a beacon of hope, distant at first but growing closer and more reachable the more he considered it. But to come home to the realisation that Jen had someone else…

He remembered a recent quote about making sure the light at the end of a tunnel wasn't an express train coming your way, and smiled grimly.

Changed locks weren't going to stop him. He'd show the usurper who owned this house. He'd break into the place. It wouldn't be the first time he'd forced one of the old casement windows open and clambered inside.

He glanced across the lane and noticed that the old block of holiday flats had been demolished in his absence. Sign of the times, but at least it meant no nosy neighbour would be watching his escapade. The houses on either side were only used in holiday time, so he'd have a clear go.

The effort of forcing the window lock on the bedroom was tougher than he remembered and in the end he gave up. Then he walked around the house to try others, testing the sliding doors from the front patio although he knew they'd be bolted inside as well as locked. The kitchen window gave a little and, ignoring the protests of his injured shoulder, he heaved against it and felt it move again. Then a shadow fell across him, dark and menacing. He ducked and something crashed against his shoulder. The world went black.

'Don't try to get up because you can't.'

Angus registered the words and, as more tendrils of consciousness returned, worked out where he was—flat on the ground beneath the window with a ten-ton weight on his back. He tried to get up anyway, and found the voice had been correct—he couldn't.

'Get off me!' he demanded, grass poking into his right eye and his mouth, the pain in his shoulder now scream-ing instead of throbbing.

'No way, mate. You're staying right where you are until the fuzz arrives. I've already rung them so they won't be long. If the burglar's been and gone they might take days to answer a call, but they hardly ever catch a real live perp so they'll trip over themselves to get their hands on you.'

Angus shifted his head so the grass he'd cut so often wasn't pressing into his mouth. It was short, he thought irrelevantly. Was Jenessa's new man cutting it?

'I'm not a burglar,' he said carefully. 'I'm the owner and I couldn't get the key to work.' He wondered if his captor, a youngish man from the sound of his voice, knew Jenessa. He amended his statement just in case. 'Part-owner. I've been away. My wife—ex-wife—lives here.'

The body on his back shifted slightly and, if anything, settled on him more heavily.

'Oh, yeah! And what's your name, then?'

'Angus McLeod.'

His words were drowned out by the shrill siren of the police car, approaching with all the cacophony expected at a major bank robbery. The body rose slightly and settled again, definitely more heavily—and higher, near his shoulder. The world went black again.

At least he was up the right way when he came to this time, and not on the grass. In fact, when he managed to have a look around he discovered he was now inside his old home, in the living room, a large open space the width of the cottage. Only, instead of the ocean view he should have from this comfortable two-seater lounge, there were two frowning faces peering down at him.

'You OK, then?' the older one asked. 'I found your passport in your bag, checked you were who you said you were, phoned your ex-wife and confirmed it was OK to let you in. Not that you can blame the lad for thinking the worst. Stupid thing to do, trying to break into a house, even if it is your own. Neigbours are sure to be suspicious, especially if you're a stranger to them.'

Again Angus heard words he couldn't totally comprehend, although this time it was pain not emotion clouding his brain. The man was in a uniform—police—so that was OK. The other face, scowling at him now, was less conciliatory. Presumably he was 'the lad'. He looked more like someone the police should be apprehending—shaven head, unhealthy-looking skin, blue stains of a tattoo visible above the ragged neckline of his T-shirt.

Angus turned back to the policeman and picked out the only piece of information that seemed relevant right then.

'You phoned Jenessa? Is she coming home?'

He hoped he didn't sound as pathetically anxious as he felt. When he'd ducked, the lad's wallop had landed on his injured shoulder which was now sending urgent messages of severe pain shafting upwards into his brain. When Jenessa came home she'd bring her bag, have something in it which would put him out of his misery.

'She'll come as soon as she can get away, and in the meantime I'm to look after you,' the young man replied. He seemed to relish the prospect and, confused as he was, Angus was still able to conjure up a variety of meanings to the words 'look after you'.

None of them was good.

'Are you also staying?' he asked the policeman, hope disappearing as the man shook his head.

'Best be off. You never know, someone might apprehend a real burglar for me to arrest.'

He held out his hand towards Angus, who took it and shook it, although the action cost him a stab of hot, sharp agony and made his head spin dizzily again.

'I don't suppose a cup of tea could be included in the "looking after" scenario?' he asked faintly, settling his head gently on the headrest and closing his eyes.

Footsteps on polished wooden floor told him the youth was moving towards the kitchen. Seemed to know his way around.

Surely…

No! Not Jenessa and a shaven-headed toy-boy! Never!

He shifted warily, easing himself forward, and wondered if the pain meant he'd damaged the skin graft, ripped open partially healed suture lines. The youth returned with a mug and plonked it down on the small table beside the lounge.

'I put sugar in it. Good for shock they say, though I didn't hit you hard enough for you to keep conking out like that. Were you putting it on for the copper?'

He had seated himself in a chair across from Angus, sitting upright, belligerence radiating from him like science fiction death rays.

'I've got a bad shoulder,' Angus explained. 'Thanks for the tea.'

He picked up the mug and sipped at the sweet, strong liquid, relishing the heat. The youth watched and the silence deepened into an uncomfortable heaviness.

'So, you know I'm Angus—who are you?' Angus said, more to lighten the atmosphere than any urge to know his assailant better.

'I'm Stick.'

Great silence-breaker. Do I now say 'Stick who' or let it go at that? Angus took another sip of tea, realised it was mentally comforting but doing little for his physical torment. He remembered he had some painkillers in his bag. He wouldn't have to wait for Jen.

'The policeman said he found my passport in my bag. Do you know where he left it? The bag, not the passport?'

Stick jerked his head towards the bench between the living room and the kitchen but made no move to fetch the bag. Angus considered the advisability of standing up, decided he'd have to some time and raised himself slowly out of the chair.

Once again, the image that swam into his vision as consciousness seeped back was of two faces peering down at him, one more anxious than the other—too anxious, too pale against the all-concealing white coat she was still wearing over her civvies.

She was talking, something about being sorry and forgetting about the locks, and…

Her voice was trembling, her distress so palpable he forced himself to speak.

'I'm OK, Jen,' he managed to say, touching her hand to reassure her. 'Banged up my shoulder. Pain's bad but I'm OK. Nearly better.'

Then he stared up at her face—knowing he was staring but unable to stop himself. She looked so beautiful—even more so than his memories. Her shoulder-length, dark hair fell forward, making her face seem thinner, more elongated, accentuating the lovely shape of her brown eyes, highlighting her strong cheekbones.

As he watched, a faint colour washed up from her neck and he saw her pale lips move, not in a smile but in speech.

Very practical speech.

'Let me have a look,' she said. 'Your right shoulder, is it? Can you roll over? Here, Jason, help me undo his shirt then turn him.'

Angus realised he was on a bed this time. His old bed—the big queen-size—not the meagre single in the spare room. Jenessa and Stick must have moved him, which meant the youth was stronger than he looked.

He was checking the well-developed muscles in Stick's arms when a more pleasing thought occurred to him. Would she have put him here if she had someone else sharing it with her?

He could hardly ask her. Not in front of a stranger. They flipped him over and pain whirled through his body, stupid thoughts doing the same in his head. He wanted to ask her, wanted to know if those cool fingers gently lifting his shirt had been touching—

No, he wouldn't think about that.

'Oh, Angus, what have you done to yourself? What happened?'

He heard her shock in a quick intake of air and the quavery formation of her words.

'Knife wound went bad,' he said, gasping himself as her fingers pressed on a tender spot. 'Long story, Jen, but I must have fallen on it earlier, and the nerves are acting up.'

'You mean it's hurting so much you keep passing out with the pain. I don't suppose it occurred to you to wait until the wound was properly healed before you undertook a two-day journey home?'

She spoke crossly but he could hear noises that promised pain relief—the snapping open of her bag, a rustle of plastic being stripped off an injection—then he felt the prick of a needle in his arm.

He lay still, his face pressed against the pillows, waiting. Wondering what he'd say when he eventually turned over and faced her, why it felt like coming home when really it wasn't.

Not that it was Jen he saw when he turned over. No sign of her. The watcher by the bed was the youth named Stick.

'She had to go back to the hospital. Said you'd sleep for a while after the shot and to get you something to eat when you woke up. You want some pizza? I ordered it earlier, but I can warm it in the microwave if you'd like some.' The words were standard politeness, the tone as uncordial as ever.

Angus moved tentatively, struggling to a sitting position, willing himself to remain conscious this time.

'I can warm it myself,' he said. 'Now I'm awake, there's no need for you to stay.'

Stick scowled at him.

'You won't get rid of me that easy. You're to stay on that bed—Jenessa said so—and that means you'll stay there, mate, if I have to knock you out again to make you. I'll get the grub.'

Angus watched him stalk, stiff-legged, from the room, and wondered what Jenessa had done to earn such devotion from the unprepossessing youth. Saved his life presumably. He settled back against the pillows then gingerly moved his right shoulder. It twitched and ached, but didn't stab with pain, the aggravated nerve endings still under the hypnotic effect of whatever Jen had injected into him.

'Pizza!' Stick thrust a plate at him. 'Want a drink? Coke? More tea?'

Angus realised how dry his throat was.

'Coke would be great,' he said.

His carer disappeared again, returning with a large bottle and a glass. He carefully poured the drink into the glass then set both on the bedside table, before resuming his seat on the chest Jen used for blankets.

'You back for long?' he asked, and Angus sensed it was more than making conversation. The young man really wanted to know.

'I'm not going back to Africa,' he answered, careful not to commit himself too far—wary about his wooing and winning programme now he was actually home. 'I've some problems with movement in my right hand and the last thing they need in a disaster area like that is a doctor who's less than one hundred per cent fit and able.'

'So you didn't come back because of—you know?'

Stick looked embarrassed as he asked the question, his

uncertain teenage skin and slightly protruding ears colouring to scarlet.

Because of 'you know'? The man Jenessa was seeing—the one she must have written about?

Angus quelled the anger which was rising again and tried for nonchalance.

'Oh, no!' he said, super-casual. 'Whatever Jenessa does is her business.'

'Geez! That's exactly how I'd summed you up!' Stick threw his arms up in the air in disgust, standing at the same time and pacing the room as if to release feelings too strong for immobility. 'I pegged you as a selfish bastard, for all she said you'd had your good times, and that you'd reason enough to go off her. Reason to go off her!' Scorn scoured his voice. 'All she wanted was a child— your child. So it took a bit of effort? So what?'

He paused in his pacing to glare at Angus again.

'You couldn't hack it, could you? Weak, that's what you are.'

A loud summons from the phone saved Angus from more of a tirade he could barely follow. While Stick answered it, Angus tucked into the pizza, trying to remember when he'd last eaten and what variety of airborne food it had been.

'That was Jenessa. She's asked someone to take her place at the sleep clinic and will be home shortly. She said if you want a shower to have it while I'm here in case you pass out again because she wouldn't be able to move you on her own.'

Stick delivered the message curtly enough for Angus to realise he'd possibly be left to drown if he did happen to pass out in the shower. Or would Stick's devotion to Jenessa ensure her commands were obeyed? He decided not to take the risk.

'I think I'll skip the shower. Perhaps you'd be kind enough to stand by while I move into the spare bedroom. The painkiller is still working so I shouldn't pass out again.'

'You can't use the spare bedroom.'

Angus frowned at his unlikely guardian.

'I don't want to take Jenessa's bed,' he said fretfully. 'I know the hours she works, and that she needs whatever sleep she can get. And I know how uncomfortable that couch is.'

'You should have thought of all that before you came barging back here,' Stick told him, disgust underlining the words.

Time to take control of this situation, Angus decided. Time to put this dreadful youth firmly in his place.

'I came back because I am still a part-owner of this house,' he said. 'And because the surgeon I want to see is on the Gold Coast. I did not come back to put Jenessa out of her bed but to use the spare bedroom, which, for your information and not that it is any of your business, I was using long before I went away.'

He wound up breathless after the effort of putting his case, but Stick seemed unimpressed.

'Well, you can't have the spare bedroom and that's that. It's all got ready now and, anyway, it's locked and she keeps the key herself. She had a lot of break-ins a few months back, kids most likely. That's why I got the locks changed for her and had another put on that door specially, 'cos she didn't want those filthy kids touching things in there.'

It might be easier if he blacked out again, Angus decided, wondering why on earth Jen would lock the spare bedroom and what 'things' might be in there. For one mad moment he thought she might have set up some kind

of shrine for him—missed him enough to put little gifts
he'd given her, perhaps some clothes he'd left behind...

A shrine for him?

Jenessa?

He laughed at the absurdity, shaking his head and
holding his shoulder so the movement didn't cause more
damage.

Stick watched him, contempt and uncertainty warring
in his eyes.

'It's nothing to laugh about, her being upset like that,
even in danger if they'd come when she was home, or if
she'd come home while they were still here.' He spoke
severely, and Angus, picturing Jen returning to a burglary
in progress, stopped laughing immediately.

Definitely not funny, but the locked spare bedroom still
puzzled him. Before he could ask for more details, Stick
spoke again.

'Jenessa knows she can sleep at my place any time she
likes,' he said. 'So you taking her bed won't be a problem.' He studied Angus for a moment then added, 'For
tonight.'

If it was meant to be reassuring then it missed by a
mile. Angus found he hated the thought of Jenessa, coming home tired after a long day at work, having to pack
and go out again to find a bed somewhere else. He must
have been frowning for Stick picked up on his concern.

'It's only next door,' he explained. 'I'm renting
there—me and my sister. That's how I came to know
Jenessa.' The glare returned, and with it the belligerence.
'I've been doing classes with her and everything. I know
just what to do. I'm the one who's been there for her all
this time—not you.'

Classes?

Human relationship and sex education? If Jen was running sleep clinics as a sideline to her work as a GP, then she could quite easily have offered classes for teenagers as well. Angus looked more closely at Stick. He'd sounded aggrieved, almost jealous. But if he was jealous, wouldn't it be of the man in Jenessa's life now, not the one who had been there? The ex?

Angus registered the turmoil of his thoughts and closed his eyes, deciding he'd put his inability to understand simple English down to the fact he was still convalescent. If you added the rigours of the long flight, plus the pain of being knocked out, sat on, interviewed by the police and generally rendered even more disabled, then a tad of confusion wasn't so surprising. He'd go back to sleep, that's what he'd do.

Not easy when all his senses were on alert, warning him of an alien presence in the room. He sneaked a quick look and caught Stick hovering at the end of the bed, staring at him in a way that made him feel even more uncomfortable.

'If you live next door, why don't you go home?' Angus complained. 'I promise you I'm not going anywhere tonight. Even if I did have the strength to get off this bed, you'd probably notice me crawling out the door and down the street.'

'I told Jenessa I'd stay,' Stick argued, settling the matter by slumping bonelessly back onto the chest. He folded his arms and continued to regard Angus with the intensity of a gaoler, keeping watch over a dangerous prisoner.

Or a murderer, waiting for his victim to fall asleep before plunging a knife into a handy intercostal space.

One of the films Angus had half watched on the plane had featured just such a scenario. He decided not to go to sleep just yet and reached out to pour himself another Coke.

There was caffeine in Coke which should keep him awake. He drank it but his taste buds must have been inactivated by Stick's intent surveillance, and the liquid was flat and tasteless.

And not as full of caffeine as he'd hoped, for his eyelids kept drooping closed and his head dropped forward on his chest, then snapped up again as he caught himself back from the brink of sleep.

'You should lie down if you're going to go to sleep,' Stick told him. 'Probably hurt your shoulder again if you keep jerking about like that.'

Angus shot him a look which he hoped conveyed the loathing he felt for this watchdog attitude.

'I'll go to sleep when I'm good and ready,' he growled. Then he heard a car pull up outside and knew Jenessa was home. The tension drained from his body so suddenly he felt lighter than air, ready to float off the bed, to drift towards slumber, to lie back and forget—

And remember.

Voices reached into his dream, but they didn't pull him out of it. Jenessa's hand brushed across his forehead and he tried to capture it, to hold it close to his heart and tell her he still loved her, to start his wooing and winning campaign right now, no matter how many new men friends she'd acquired in his absence. But his own hand wouldn't move, his limbs too heavy, then the voices faded, the room went dark and there was only sleep.

CHAPTER TWO

JENESSA struggled off the couch, and stretched her cramped and aching back. Considering all that had happened, she'd slept surprisingly well. Was Angus awake?

She crossed the living room and opened the door to the main bedroom. He was still in bed, lying on his left side, slight rustling movements indicating he was sleeping less deeply than the previous time she'd checked. With her heart fluttering uncertainly in her chest, she studied him, pretending it was a medical appraisal yet knowing it was personal. She needed to feast her eyes on him and renew the images she carried with her every minute of the day.

Light from the window fell across his face, finding the fairer highlights in his longish, dark blond hair. His eyebrows and eyelashes were brown, close to black, dark against skin pale from what must have been a lengthy stay in hospital. She shivered, remembering how his eyes had looked when he'd finally opened them the previous afternoon. Greener than she remembered them, but glazed by pain or shock.

Or fever? Seeing the scar high up on his right shoulder, she'd wondered about fever, the wound beneath the graft so deep it suggested a mammoth battle against infection. But, no, he'd been cool to the touch, not feverish.

Closing the door again, she continued on down the short passage which led to the back entrance. On her left was the room they'd converted into a study and beyond that, on the right, the bathroom. She entered cautiously.

30

It had two-way access, this one from the hall, the other leading into the main bedroom. That door was shut and she washed quietly, unwilling to disturb the sleeper any sooner than was absolutely necessary.

The moment of reckoning would come, but she had no wish to rush to meet it.

She came out and sighed as she glanced towards yet another door, the one opposite the bathroom. Then she shook her head to banish the jumbled thoughts and returned to the kitchen.

A soft rattle from the patio told her Jason had arrived, and she walked across to let him in, smiling when she saw the white paper bag and smelled whatever delicious goodies he'd bought for her this morning.

'I'm supposed to be monitoring my weight,' she reminded him, following him through to the kitchen and watching as he filled the kettle with water and set it to boil. This Saturday morning ritual of breakfast with Jason had become a highlight in her week. She enjoyed listening to his tales of what had happened at school, and encouraged him to share his youthful philosophies.

'He still sleeping?' Jason jerked his head towards the bedroom door, and Jenessa hid a smile at the antagonism in his voice.

'Like the proverbial log,' she responded, 'although I guess the demands of nature will wake him before long. It's close to twelve hours if you count it from when I gave him the injection.'

'You glad he's home?'

Jen made the coffee—so weak is was more like coloured water—while she considered this. Her body was glad—traitorously so—but her head opted for caution.

'I suppose I'm glad he felt he had to come.'

'Oh, sh…sugar!' Jason muttered, but before she could

enquire why her reply had upset him the subject of their
conversation appeared, tall, too thin, sleep-rumpled and
pale, but definitely recognisable to every cell of her body
as Angus—the man she loved. Or had loved. No, still
loved if her physical response was any guide.

He stood there in the doorway to their bedroom, where
he'd stood a thousand times before, and looked at her,
then at Jason and once more, as if puzzled, back at her
again. Her training saw the difference in his skin colour
as it drained from pale to ashen, and she rushed towards
him, certain he was about to collapse again.

But he grasped the doorjamb and remained upright,
frowning furiously, glaring at her, his green eyes darting
fire in that white, white face.

'You're pregnant!'

He slammed the statement at her as violently as an
accusation of murder and she felt an answering frown
twitch at her eyebrows.

'Isn't that why you—?' she began. But he was speaking again, talking over her, raining the words so heavily
on her head she forgot her own question as she tried to
catch up with his bitter, damning accusations.

'And obviously found someone whose sperm could
penetrate the hamster's eggs,' he finished.

Jason darted between them, standing protectively in
front of Jenessa.

'Don't talk to her like that!' he yelled. 'Or call her
names like hamster!'

His voice cracked on the last word and Jen knew he'd
be mortified by the adolescent weakness. As Angus spun
around and disappeared back into the bedroom, she
touched Jason lightly on the shoulder, then led him back
into the kitchen and sat him on a stool.

'The hamster thing is a test,' she said gently, hiding

her grief at the realisation that Angus hadn't come home because of the baby. Her letter hadn't reached him and, from what she could make out, he was now assuming she was pregnant by someone else.

Perhaps…

'What kind of test?'

She looked at Jason, so vulnerable to hurt at seventeen, and decided that explaining a hamster test probably made as much sense as anything else had in the last fifteen hours.

'We've talked a lot about the reasons why women can't conceive, about sperm numbers and motility. Usually in IVF programmes, once it's been proven that the man's sperm is OK on all counts, then it's assumed the problem is with the woman. That's when doctors try to get sperm and egg together in the oviducts so they don't have as much chance of missing each other. If that consistently fails, they fertilise the eggs outside the womb. Sometimes they do another test and, for some reason, we did it very late in the proceedings.'

'Like, after years?'

Jenessa smiled, although there wasn't much humour in that chapter of the past, or this page of the present. But Jason's fascination with the IVF process always amused her, and she was sure he could probably give every detail of her medical history if ever asked.

'Well, not years but many, many months,' she agreed. 'Which was silly because things could have been different in the beginning. Anyway, with a hamster test, eggs are harvested from a hamster and the surrounding cell coating is removed, then they're put together with some incubated sperm and left for a few hours. It's not infallible but if the sperm don't penetrate any of the eggs, it could indicate that they won't penetrate a woman's eggs either.'

'So it wasn't your fault you couldn't get pregnant?'

Jen sighed.

'It's a no-blame situation, Jason. The whole business of not conceiving can't be put down to one partner or the other. It could be that my eggs were exceedingly tough which means if he'd had another partner this might not have been a problem for Angus. As it turned out, at the time when the hamster test was done Angus's sperm lacked penetration, but for all we know he may have had a virus at the time, something that made a difference to his sperm then but not earlier—and definitely not later.'

She glanced towards the bedroom door, coffee and sweet pastries forgotten.

'I'll have to go and talk to him,' she said. 'That's where things went wrong before. I headed along the track to getting pregnant, test after test, treatment after treatment, so focussed on my own goal I never stopped to consider how Angus felt about it. I imagined he felt as I did, but in the end I discovered it was my obsession, not ours. In the last months there was no communication between us about what was surely the most important thing in both our lives.' She smiled bleakly. 'He told me, when he eventually called a halt to the madness, that he didn't want a child—hadn't ever wanted one.'

'So what's going to happen now?'

'That's what I'd like to know.' Angus appeared on cue, although Jen doubted he'd heard her part in the conversation. He didn't come into the kitchen but stood, glowering, in the hall. 'If you think I'm going to shift out of this house so your lover can live with you, you've another think coming. The house is half mine—you go and live with him.'

'She hasn't got a lover!' Jason retorted, before Jenessa could stop him. 'The baby's—'

'Not happy about all this argument,' she interjected, her mind racing along a path of its own, wondering if fate had given her a second chance to keep the baby's father from knowing it was his. Until she'd sorted out her own feelings about Angus's return—about Angus himself—and how he felt about her. After all, she *had* written to tell him—wasn't that enough?

'Angus, come in and sit down. Have something to eat and drink.'

'She must have had a lover at some time!' he said, to Jason not to her, although his gaze was on her, raking down her body, his eyes so hot with his anger she could almost feel the scornful appraisal—certainly felt its heat.

'Why *did* you come home?' she asked, trying to cool the emotion zapping through the air as he continued to hover and glare. 'Because of your shoulder? Is it all right this morning? Do you need more medication?'

'Oh, stop rabbiting on about my shoulder,' Angus muttered, sweeping into the kitchen and seizing the coffee-pot, reaching automatically for a mug. 'Is this coffee?' he demanded as he poured the pale liquid then stared at it in disbelief.

'It's not good for pregnant women to have too much caffeine so I compromise on strength.' Trying for cool and calm despite the heat and provocation. 'There's instant if you want something stronger.'

'Something stronger, like a double whisky, might be the answer,' he said gruffly, spooning sugar into the dubious brew and stirring it with sharp jerky movements. He opened the bakery bag and pulled out a pastry. 'This mine?'

Jenessa wasn't going to contradict him and Jason, perhaps sensing the tension, so tangible it was hard to breathe, had gone quiet. Jen picked up her coffee and walked through to the living room, slumping down on to the couch that had caused the back pain she was still enduring.

Big mistake. It drew Angus's attention to it, and to the tangle of sheets bunched at one end.

'Did you sleep there?' he demanded. 'In your condition?'

'I could hardly have slept here in any other condition,' she snapped, tired of playing peace-keeper. 'There was someone in my bed.'

'He said, Stick said, you could stay next door.'

Angus was frowning at her as if he was genuinely concerned—or perhaps because he was as thrown by the situation as she was.

'You'd lost consciousness three times in the space of a couple of hours,' she reminded him tartly. 'What I should have done was had you carted off to hospital, but it seemed a trifle unwelcoming on your first night home.'

'You stayed here to keep an eye on me?' He came closer and sat down in a lounge chair opposite the couch, so dear and familiar yet so angry with her, so lost to her, she wanted to cry.

Not that she intended showing that kind of weakness in front of him. One glimpse of a crack in her defences and he'd strike.

She shrugged to show how little it mattered.

'Seemed like the right thing to do.' She turned her head towards the kitchen where Jason was still perched on a stool, his chest, shoulders and head visible above the dividing bench. 'Is there another pastry there, Jason? I'm starving.'

That should add to the 'couldn't care less' impression.

She glanced towards Angus to see if it had worked and caught his look of mortification.

'If they were in the white paper bag, then I ate the last one. I didn't think—'

'I'll go get some more.'

Jason was off his stool and out the door within seconds, his relief at finding an excuse to escape so obvious that Jen smiled.

'Should we start again?' she said, studying her ex-husband, seeing the lines of suffering in his face, the gauntness caused by weight loss. Feeling her heart clench as she imagined what he'd been through, then flutter as she realised he was really home. Play it cool, she reminded herself. 'I could begin with hello, how are you and, without rabbiting on about your shoulder, ask what happened.'

Angus barely heard her questions, his mind struggling with its own confusion. He stared at her, his eyes drawn to her face, so serene in spite of the short flares of temper she'd shown earlier. He had to come to terms with this. Had to take time to absorb the reality and readjust his mental images of his homecoming. Perhaps then he could work out what to do next. He studied the woman he'd hoped to woo and win.

She was wearing a long, fine knit garment that showed the heaviness of her enlarged breasts and clung to the bulge as if to accentuate her pride in her achievement of pregnancy. He recalled his shock as he'd stood in the doorway and seen that shape for the first time, certain his mind had been playing tricks on him, superimposing another of the beautiful paintings he'd admired a few days ago—one of a pregnant Madonna—onto the real Jenessa. His fantasies coming to life!

But she was real, not a fantasy. Not only real but unbearably beautiful. And if that wasn't enough, to his shame his body seemed to find her sexy, his groin stirring as it hadn't stirred in a long, long time. Forget your groin—get a grip, man, he urged himself. He thought back to his arrival, to the phone call he'd made and the conversation which hadn't made much sense. Somewhere in it there had to be a clue.

'What letter?' he asked her.

Her surprise was obvious, and she frowned at him, her smooth, broad brow wrinkling.

'You said you sent a letter,' he persisted, but he guessed she was stalling now, that she knew what letter and was weighing up her answer in her mind. Why?

'I wrote, oh, about three months ago, maybe longer, to tell you I was pregnant.' She smoothed the material of her dress over the bulge as she answered, teasing out small wrinkles as if appearance was important. 'I didn't realise for ages.' Now she raised her head and met his eyes, a rueful kind of smile hovering around her lips. 'I mean, after all those months of science doing its best, it wasn't exactly what I'd expect from a one-night stand.'

'A one-night stand?' His shoulder hurt as he lurched to his feet, too furious to remain seated. 'You had a quick fling with a stranger and this happened? When? A day after I left? A week? Or did you do the decent thing and wait a month?' He glared at her, unable to believe the Jenessa he had known could—

'It was the baby business, wasn't it? That's why you did it? Probably why you insisted we divorce. Once you knew my sperm had failed the test, you went out and latched onto someone else's.'

She was watching him as he stormed around the room—he could feel it even when he wasn't looking at her. He spun to face her, to catch her watching him, and saw she wasn't smiling now. If anything, she looked ill, her eyes so full of hurt he felt her pain like a stab-wound in his heart.

It was his use of those wretched words, 'the baby business', which had struck the blow. He'd wanted to retract them as soon as they were spoken, remembering how devastated she'd been the first time he'd unwittingly used the phrase with which he'd mentally labelled their IVF debacle.

He stopped pacing and held out his hands in supplication.

'I'm sorry, Jen, that was unfair. I know how much you wanted a child. I should be happy for you that you're fulfilling your dream, not roaring at you.'

He said the words she needed to hear, but they tore him apart. Surely, if he loved her, he *should* be happy for her. So why did he want to murder someone? Why was rage, not happiness, his foremost emotion?

She gazed up at him, her eyes huge and dark in her pale face, her body language suggestive of a wild animal trapped in the mesmeric glare of a hunter's lights. She hadn't bought the 'happy'!

'*Can* you be happy for me?' she asked, and he dropped back into the chair, knowing what he should reply but trying to rationalise his tumultuous emotions.

Take them one at a time.

Not happy, certainly.

Angry still, but beyond the anger something more insidious, as destructive as the festering organisms that had invaded his knife wound.

Jealousy! That was what he felt. It churned in his intestines with the acrid bitterness of bile.

'It's what you've always wanted,' he said, when the silence had stretched too long for comfort.

'But not what you wanted, Angus,' she said sadly. 'My dream, not yours, and it broke up our marriage.'

The turmoil diminished, instinct telling him to comfort her, but the shadow of an unknown man now stood between them—the father of a child that should have been his.

'I suppose everyone going into marriage expects to have children some time, although I certainly didn't get married for that reason. When it didn't work that way for us, it wasn't important to me. What I hated was seeing you upset each time the system failed. Hell, you know the statistics as well as I do. A significant percentage of relationships don't survive unsuccessful IVF treatments.'

She stared at him as if trying to assess his mood, to see past the placating words he'd used to shield his irrational emotions.

'But in the end you said you didn't want a child,' she reminded him, bringing up the statement that had driven the final spike into the heart of their marriage.

'Not so badly I'd not only destroy our marriage to achieve it, but kill whatever respect and friendship had survived as well,' he countered. 'That's all I meant. Well, not quite all. If you think back to before it started, when we were going out together and first married. I always believed we were special—as a couple. That we were complete within ourselves. I suppose I wondered if having a child would change all that, although, in the end, it was not having a child that did it.'

The words sounded pathetic in his ears but she seemed to accept them, nodding her head so her hair moved and the sun caught glints of burnished copper in the darkness.

'And if it had happened—if I *had* become pregnant— right at the end of all the treatment when things were so strained and awkward between us, how would you have felt?'

How would he have felt? He was trying to decide, to think back and imagine if such news would have been a welcome relief, a cause for celebration or a new chain around his neck, when she answered for him, or offered one reply.

'Trapped?'

'I suppose so,' he said slowly, 'although it's all so hypothetical, Jen. Once you change one variable, so much else can change. It's hard to say.'

She nodded, as if his answer had been what she'd expected, rubbed her hands across her stomach in a strangely protective gesture, then looked up at him and smiled.

'So, enough of me. Tell me about your shoulder.'

Enough of her? When she was sitting there in front of him, hugely pregnant with a fatherless baby, and he was being eaten alive by jealousy and lusting after her at the same time?

He dragged his attention from the deep cleft between her breasts, where their fullness showed above the neckline of her dress, and decided a change in conversation might not be such a bad idea.

'It was bad luck—a case of being in the wrong place at the wrong time. We had a plane come in with supplies and I'd helped unload it then stayed back to do an inventory when the others left. Some kid, high on drugs, came in looking for more supplies. He stabbed me in the shoulder, I yelled, and one of the security guards came rushing in and shot the kid.'

'Shot the kid? Shot a young drug addict?'

A tremor in Jen's voice showed her reaction. Damn it! He should have edited this story, left out that example of the callous disregard for life he'd witnessed again and again in seven months in the drought- and war-torn country.

'He didn't die,' he lied to reassure her. 'In fact, he ran away, far more mobile than I was.'

'And was someone there to stitch you up? What happened next? That scar is from a skin graft, not a simple stab wound.'

She sounded concerned for him and his silly heart reacted with a faster beat, although his head told him she'd been equally concerned for his assailant.

'One of the French doctors irrigated the wound, pumped it full of antibiotics and stitched me up, but some dire organism had already taken hold. I was so feverish by the following morning they diagnosed gangrene and loaded me onto the plane which had brought in the supplies.'

'Gangrene?' Jenessa breathed the word, and shook her head as if the movement might dismiss it. 'Given the use of antibiotics, can wounds turn gangrenous so quickly?'

She looked across the space which separated them and wondered why she should still feel his pain, should care so deeply what happened to him. Would it be like this for ever?

'Apparently! I don't remember much about it,' Angus continued, oblivious to her reaction to his tale. 'I was delirious, totally out of it, and only began remembering things after I'd been in hospital in Paris for a week or so. By then they'd excised most of the diseased tissue but they kept the wound open, washing it and cutting away more disgusting flesh until they finally decided they had the lot. I had antibiotics dripping into my veins, which probably helped, and eventually they took skin from my thigh and patched up the hole they'd dug, waited until they were sure the graft had taken, then sent me home.'

A wounded shoulder had brought him home, not a letter from me! Not the news that she was pregnant with his child. She'd accepted that earlier when he'd asked about the letter, but the disappointment was no less with this confirmation.

'Home, not back to Africa?' she asked, determined to keep the conversation on something other than her condition.

Angus used his left hand to grip his right forearm and lift it a few inches into the air, then closed his fingers into a loose fist.

'There was muscle and nerve damage from the initial wound, and cutting away the infected area made that worse. The specialists assure me I'll get full use of it eventually, but at the moment I haven't a full range of movement.'

He paused, and eyed her assessingly, before adding, 'That's why I came back, Jen. It wasn't to throw your life into chaos, but because Allan Greene is here. He's the best man I know for those kind of ligament and tendon repairs.'

Jenessa heard the words but knew him well enough to believe there had been a lot left unsaid.

About his injury? Was it worse than he'd made out?

She shrugged off her doubts. One thing was clear—his primary motive for coming here was to consult Allan, not because he still considered this house his home. It was convenient, nothing more, and she could stop the wild daydreams in which, somehow, they would make a family. In fact, her earlier instinct had probably been correct. It would be better all around if Angus didn't know she was carrying his child. That way, he wouldn't be forced to make a decision about sharing the parenting, or acting as father to a baby he hadn't wanted.

The front door rattled, slid back and Jason returned, another small white paper bag held triumphantly aloft.

'The almond croissants were out of the oven that time,' he said, directing the words to Jen and studiously ignoring Angus. 'I know they're your favourite so I bought you two. I'll make fresh coffee.'

He plunged across the room into the kitchen, and she heard splashing as he filled the kettle.

Across from her, Angus had turned to watch Jason's actions and scowl at the young man's unsuspecting back.

'Does he spend all his spare time here?' Angus asked, hissing the question at her in a very carrying undertone. If she hadn't known better she'd have thought he was jealous, but Angus was far too confident to be jealous of a seventeen-year-old kid.

'A lot of it. His girlfriend works at McDonald's so he's at a loose end weekends when he's not surfing,' she explained, then she remembered how much she appreciated Jason's company and help. 'In fact, I doubt I'd have got through the last few months without him.'

Angus's frown deepened. He opened his mouth, then shut it again, evidently thinking the better of whatever he'd intended saying. No doubt it had been something cutting about Jason's attentions.

Well, she'd occasionally worried about his devotion herself, but he seemed to enjoy being with her, and she'd certainly needed someone on whom she could rely— someone to talk to when her thoughts were too depressing to handle on her own.

Jason brought her coffee over to her and set it on the small table with a plate bearing the two croissants, then he hovered, as if uncertain of his place in her life now Angus had returned.

'Are you staying?' she asked him, not wanting him to feel uncomfortable or in the way.

'I've got time,' he offered. 'You haven't done your exercises and we were going to put the frieze up on the walls, but if you need to talk to him I can come back some other time.'

Angus wasn't sure if he was angered or amused by the youngster's attitude. The 'him' had been accompanied by a jerk of the shaven head in Angus's direction, but otherwise Stick—or Jason, as Jenessa called him—had ignored him.

'We might leave the frieze until tomorrow,' Jen replied. 'And I promise I'll do the exercises as soon as I've eaten. In the meantime, isn't the surf up? I looked out an hour or so ago and the waves were building nicely. With the tide coming in, you should get some good rides.'

Tactful, that's what she was, his ex-wife. She'd not wounded Stick's feelings with an outright refusal of his company, and had offered an alternative she must know he'd enjoy. In fact, if his shoulder hadn't been affected by yesterday's rough handling, he might have tried to catch a wave himself.

'You can go, too,' Jenessa said to him, reading his mind with uncanny accuracy. 'If your shoulder's up to it.'

'It's not,' he said, nodding to Stick as the teenager left the house. 'Besides, I'd rather watch you do your exercises. The shape you're in it should be fascinating.'

She glowered at him, then chuckled.

'You're right. I'm about as graceful as a baby elephant, and less co-ordinated.'

The sound of her laughter filtered into his senses and

he gazed at her, seeing not the pregnant stranger but the Jen who'd been his soul-mate for so long. His friend, his lover, his wife!

'I hope you've been able to laugh through all of this,' he said, praying she'd understand his feelings went deeper than the words. 'That you've been able to enjoy the pregnancy you wanted so badly, not had your pleasure marred by being worried or concerned.'

She stared at him as if surprised, then shook her head.

'For the first four months I didn't know,' she admitted. 'Oh, I was tired all the time, cranky as all hell, but I thought it was just a combination of things. The divorce, you being gone, the drugs I'd been on working their way out of my system. When Dick Hollingsworth suggested I might be pregnant, I roared with laughter. Then I was shocked, then...'

She was looking sad again, but he had to know how she'd felt when she'd realised the outcome of that 'one-night stand' she'd mentioned earlier.

'Then?' he prompted.

She smiled and shrugged, and her lovely face twisted into a wry grimace.

'Confused, I guess! Excited, but confused.'

Confused because the bastard who'd fathered the child never wanted to see her again, Angus surmised. That could be the only explanation.

'Did you tell him?' he demanded.

'Tell him?'

'The father of the baby? Did you tell him you were pregnant? For heaven's sake, Jen, you must have known his name. Must have met him a few times before you leapt into bed with him.'

Again she smiled, only this time there was no shrug, just an awful sadness in her eyes.

'Oh, I knew his name,' she whispered. 'And I tried to tell him. But in the end I think it's for the best that he doesn't know. I know from my own experience, it's better to have one loving parent than two people held together by the bonds of a mutual child.'

Angus sighed, unable to believe the situation or that whoever had fathered Jenessa's child would not want to be part of her life for ever. He knew she couldn't be happy, heading towards the birth of this longed-for baby without a partner to share her joy.

'Your parents' marriage is hardly typical,' he pointed out. 'They couldn't agree on anything—right from the start when one wanted to call you Jennifer and the other Vanessa, and look what happened there. They didn't know the meaning of love, so how could they have learned to love each other? But plenty of people do make a go of things.'

'If they're in love. If they share the same dreams for the future.'

'You said that as if there's a ''but'' hanging off it. This bloke you went with, did he not want children? I can't believe you learnt so much about him in one short night.'

Jenessa smiled again, and he felt a totally inappropriate stirring in his body as if it was a special smile, like a benediction just for him.

'It wasn't a short night but a long one,' she said softly. 'And I did know him. Had known him for a while.'

Angus shot to his feet and walked out of the room, out on to the patio where he could look across the beach to the ocean, breathe deeply and unclench his hands which were locked so tightly that if he'd got them around the neck of that unknown blighter he'd have strangled the life out of him.

He couldn't believe it was someone he knew—that someone he knew could sleep with Jenessa once then never want to see her again. Because if she knew him then so must he, for they'd not only lived together for six years but studied together before their marriage.

Someone from work? No, the men she worked with would know about the pregnancy and the fellow would guess he was responsible. Someone they'd studied with who now lived interstate? Up here on holiday perhaps? Hadn't there been a GPs' convention at Jupiters shortly after his departure? He remembered Jen saying she may as well go—catch up with old friends.

In fact, she'd joked about getting out and about now she was single again. Joked about it as they'd showered and dressed after the night at the Sheraton—or had it been in the car as she drove him to the airport?

He'd been distinctly peeved, mainly because he'd been feeling maudlin and upset that he was finally leaving her. In fact, in the afterglow of a night of good sex, he'd been wondering if it might have been possible for them to start again. Not right then, of course, but when he returned—in a couple of years.

And she'd been organising her future love-life!

He watched a board-rider paddle out through the surf to join a group of four sitting astride their boards, waiting for a set. He heard their shouts, and saw them lean forward, moving in ballet-like unison, then stand as they caught the swelling wave, slight movements of their feet and ankles steering the short boards through the green curl of the water.

That's what he needed—time out from this confusion. Sun and surf, a board beneath his feet.

He swung back towards the doors and stuck his head through into the room.

'Is my board still in the shed?' he asked.

'Where else?' she said, not smiling now at all.

CHAPTER THREE

BY THE time Angus had wiped his surfboard free of cob-
webs and dust he was exhausted. Taking it out in his
condition, that would be suicidal. The alternative was to
go back into the house and cope with his contrary feelings towards Jenessa. Once beyond the breakers he could
just sit on the board and think this situation through—
work out what he was going to do, how he was going to
cope with this unexpected development and his reaction
to it.

But would he make it past the breakers?

Probably not.

He clasped his left arm around the board and lifted it
awkwardly, his less dominant side unfamiliar with the
dynamics of board-carrying.

'You won't make it past the breakers in your condition.'

As he reached the front patio Jenessa spoke his
thoughts aloud, and the quick anger, not part of his usual
self, rose again.

'I thought you were the one with the condition,' he
said with a nasty leer at her distended belly. Then he let
the board slide to the ground as the anger faded as fast
as it had risen. 'I'd already realised that,' he admitted.
'Actually, I thought it would help me think. It's all been
a bit much for me, coming home to find you pregnant. I
know it shouldn't be affecting me like this, that it's none
of my business what you do with your life, but…'

She came closer and slid her hand through his arm.

'But it takes a bit of getting used to. I know, it's the same for me. I felt ill when I saw your shoulder and realised what you'd been through. We've cared about each other for a long time and that's a habit that won't suddenly go away, Angus. We just have to adjust to the new parameters in our lives. Now, instead of battling against the waves, would you like a sedate walk along the beach? That's if you're not embarrassed to be seen with someone who sticks out a lot in front and from behind, I'm told, waddles like a duck.'

He could feel the weight of her body against his side, and the tautness of the skin beneath her clinging dress. He wanted to touch her, feel the new shape of her, but knew he couldn't take the risk. For one thing it would upset her, and for another he might not want to stop.

'A walk sounds good,' he said gruffly, helping her step over the low wall around the patio and steadying her as they crossed the soft sand. Once on firmer ground, she moved as if to withdraw her hand from his arm, but he pressed his elbow against his side to keep the contact with her.

They walked in silence, falling into an easy rhythm, nodding to those who were strolling or striding in the other direction. He noticed people smiling, some enviously, others with a kind of knowing complicity, as if Jenessa's obvious pregnancy was a reaffirmation of all that was good in life. He walked a little straighter, proud of the attention shown to the gorgeous, heavily pregnant woman by his side.

Which was foolish, and quite possibly dangerous as well.

'I'll phone Phil Sawyers when we get back to the house. I can probably camp at his place for a few days until I know what I'm doing.'

'Phil left for England last week,' Jen told him. 'And you're welcome to stay with me. After all, it's as much your house as it is mine.'

True, but could he bear to be so close to her, given the circumstances? He remembered the plan he'd stated so confidently to Alain and felt more hollow laughter rattling inside his head. His mind searched for objections to get him gracefully out of this arrangement.

'You can't keep sleeping on the couch, and I've never fitted on it.'

She eased her hand free and moved a little apart.

'The bed from the spare room is in the shed. I'll get Jason to bring it back inside and take my turn on it.'

'The spare room's locked, or so your youthful guard informed me.'

He realised he hadn't found out why, and looked at her, waiting for an explanation.

'I've been decorating it.' A faint blush crept into her cheeks, as if she'd enjoyed the task but was slightly embarrassed by her pleasure in it. 'The bed was in the way so we shifted it out. If you're looking for a job, the locum I'd arranged to come in for three months has just let me down. If you have to stay on the coast to see Allan regularly, and you're interested…'

'Switching the conversation, Jen?'

The colour in her cheeks deepened, and when she looked up at him he saw the uncertainty in her eyes.

'Well, I know you're not interested in all the baby stuff and you'll probably laugh when you see it. I kind of overdid things I expect, but…'

He found his heart contracting into a small hard lump but hid his pain, touching his forefinger very gently to her nose.

'Why shouldn't you? You'd waited so long for this to

happen. Do you think I don't understand that? I *am* happy for you, believe me.'

It was a lie, of course. He wasn't at all happy for her. Perhaps in a way he was, but it certainly wasn't his overwhelming emotion. Deep in his tortured soul, jealousy still reigned supreme.

Jenessa eyed him warily, then turned and began to walk back towards the house, trying to guess what was going on inside his head. He was saying all the right things, but did he mean them? Considering he'd gone along with the IVF procedures for a year, before telling her he hadn't ever wanted a child, she didn't know what to believe. Although, to give him his due, he probably was happy for her.

Time to get back to the conversational switch—far easier to cope with practical matters than delve into emotional stuff. She faced him as he caught up and fell into step beside her.

'Do you want a job?'

'Providing I've got backup for any manoeuvres where I can't use my arm, and the others are willing to take over when I have an appointment elsewhere, I could stand in for you. When had you expected your locum to start?'

She hesitated. Perhaps it was foolish, mentioning the job—tying him here longer than was absolutely necessary. But she'd had to offer him accommodation in his own house, and to have him around the place when she stopped work...

The two of them together, all day every day?

No way.

'The locum was starting Monday, working with me for a week to get to know the routine and meet some of the regulars, then on his own from the following week.'

'So, you'd want me to start Monday?'

A curiously flat question, with no sign of how he felt about the prospect. Jenessa considered her reply, wondering if she'd misread a signal somewhere.

'Well, not necessarily. After all, you already know the routine, and you're not fit. You have to make appointments and arrangements of your own. Jack and Neville, the chap who took your place, know the locum's pulled out and they're prepared to take on the extra work until the agency can find someone else.'

'Oh, no, I can start Monday,' Angus assured her. His mind had scooted ahead, picturing his return to his old workplace, his friends' surprise, their greetings and delight. The gossip.

It was an odds-on bet he'd know the father of Jenessa's child by Monday afternoon *and* learn more about him as the days passed. Kathy in Reception wouldn't have let a mystery like this lie dormant. She'd have ferreted out the details, while Jack usually knew everything that went on within a radius of a hundred kilometres.

Yes, Angus would soon learn whatever there was to know about the rat-fink.

He smiled in satisfaction and saw Jen smile back at him. No doubt she'd assumed he was pleased about the job. Which he was, of course. Quite apart from the information-gathering aspect of going to work, there was the escape it offered. Her lush body was already exerting far too much influence on his so the last thing he wanted was to be spending more time with her once she stopped work. Wooing and winning weren't entirely forgotten, but would have to be relegated to the back burner until he had time to untangle his confusion over the present situation.

Stick—or maybe he'd join Jenessa and call him

Jason—was walking up the beach, his board tucked casually under his arm. He ignored Angus but cocked an eyebrow at Jenessa.

'Exercises?'

'I suppose so.' She sighed. 'You get dry while I change. See you back at the house in a few minutes.'

Angus watched the youth's retreating back for a second, then turned to Jenessa.

'You must know how important exercise is. Why does he have to keep reminding you?'

She smiled as she looked up, but she met his eyes squarely as she admitted, 'Because I hate it. I know I have to do it but it's so boring. The only thing that makes it even remotely bearable is Jason acting as my partner.'

'Acting as your partner?'

She'd walked on when she'd finished talking so he had to hurry to catch up and ask his question.

'Yes, doing them with me. Lamaze started all of that— at least, I think it was him. He believed that if the man was to be more than a cipher in the delivery room then he should be part of the whole process and know about the breathing and stretching and pressure points which rubbing can relieve.'

Angus was so staggered by this statement he didn't steady her as she clambered over the low wall, mutely watching her sway as she regained her balance on the other side.

'But Lamaze was talking about the father's participation. You're not telling me— You don't mean—'

He must have been yelling, for Jen swung back to face him.

'That Jason—? Oh, don't be so stupid, Angus. Am I the kind of woman who'd take advantage of a kid like that?'

She stormed away from him and he shook his head, aware he no longer knew what kind of woman she was.

'Then why does he help you with the exercises?' he persisted as he entered the house and caught sight of her disappearing into the bedroom.

'Because he's agreed to be with me at the birth,' she snapped, then she slammed the door shut behind her.

'But he's little more than a child—he can't go through an experience like that. It would put him off sex for life.'

He opened the door and walked in—an automatic re-action—then stopped dead when he saw her, clad only in a bra and tiny lacy bikini pants, her skin pale and tight across her stomach, beautiful in a way he didn't fully understand.

'I'm sorry. I shouldn't have barged in like that.' He was backing out as he floundered through the apology. 'But have you thought this through? Does he know what he's in for?'

She smiled at him and he decided he'd never seen anything as beautiful as the proudly pregnant woman standing in front of him. His mouth went dry and he had to force himself to listen to her when she answered.

'He's seen films, been up to the hospital to check out the delivery suites and come with me when I've had a scan. He's seventeen, nearly eighteen, old enough to make the choice himself.'

Angus took another backward step and shut the door behind him. He'd heard of children as young as five join-ing other members of the family to watch the arrival of a new sibling. He wasn't certain how he felt about it, but supposed it was natural enough.

Yet...

'At his age I'd have been useless. In fact, I'd have thrown up!' he yelled through the closed door, and, having vented his spleen, he wandered into the kitchen, found the instant coffee and put the kettle on to boil. Maybe a caffeine jolt was what he needed. He pulled open the door of the refrigerator.

'There's no milk. I used the last in Jenessa's coffee.'

Angus closed the door very carefully and turned around. Stick—Jason was standing just inside the glass doors. Had he been there long? Heard the conversation?

'I'll drink it black,' he growled at the intrusive youth, then memories of himself at that age surfaced and with them his disbelief that the lad intended being Jenessa's 'partner' at the birth.

'She tells me you're going to be with her when she has the baby. Are you sure about that? I mean, it's not the same as seeing it on a film or TV where you're removed from it. In real life, it's a very messy business.'

Stick edged further into the living room and dropped into a cross-legged sitting position on the rug.

'I know all that but someone's got to be there for her. It's not as if her parents care—or you!'

'I do care about her and of course I'd be there for her if she wanted me,' Angus argued, but all he received in reply was a look of pure scorn.

He was about to tell Stick exactly what he thought of him when Jenessa reappeared, clad this time in clinging bike shorts and a big short-sleeved shirt that looked suspiciously like an old one of his.

'All ready?' she said gaily to Stick as she crossed the room, without casting a glance in Angus's direction. She lowered herself gingerly to the floor, moving close to the lad then crossing her legs so their knees were almost touching.

'Start with breathing,' Stick told her. 'Breathe in and

feel your ribcage expand, then let go all your tension as you breathe out.'

Stick shot a glare at Angus over Jenessa's head and Angus knew he was being held responsible for the tension, but he was fascinated by the performance, by the young adolescent-man taking such devoted care of the pregnant woman.

He made his coffee and perched on a stool, sipping at it while he watched the pair go through the relaxation part of the exercises. Stick anticipated every move Jenessa had to make, shifting cushions to put behind her as she lay back, holding her limbs as she flexed and re-laxed.

Angus felt his own tension growing as Jenessa's eased. Although Stick's touch was as impersonal as a doctor's, it aggravated Angus. He couldn't help but feel he should have been the one doing this with her, for all his prot-estations of not wanting a child.

It seemed to go on for ever, techniques to strengthen the obliques, the lower abdominals, the outer and inner thighs. Stick not only knew what to do, but obviously had learned enough to know how the movements worked and why the various muscles would be needed.

'Yo, Stick! You there!'

The loud call from the patio brought it to an end, Stick standing up and hurrying to the door as if to protect Jenessa from more intrusion. There was a muted conver-sation then he turned back towards Jenessa who was ly-ing on her back, her hands crossed on her belly, breathing quietly.

'Pete's dad's ready to go, but I haven't rubbed your back,' he said, so obviously torn between pleasure and duty that Angus hid a smile.

'Go!' Jenessa ordered. 'I can live without a back rub for a day.'

Stick glanced from her to Angus, who heard the unspoken question.

'He's OK now he's had a little yell,' Jenessa told the lad. 'Off you go.'

This time he obeyed, calling goodbye as he slid the door closed behind him.

'He can also rub backs, if he hasn't lost the knack,' Angus offered, although a little put out that Jen would talk about him in that fashion.

She sat up and looked at him.

'Would you? I must admit, my back's killing me. The couch definitely hasn't improved.' She hesitated, then smiled uncertainly. 'I'm sorry about that ''yelling'' crack, but I think he heard us arguing and he's so protective he'd have stayed home although he's been talking about going up to Brisbane for the rugby game for weeks.'

Angus left the safety of the kitchen and crossed the living room towards her. Jenessa lay down again on the rug, on her side with her legs curled up, her hand pressed against her spine between her buttock muscles and her waist.

'It's just in there and I think it needs more pressure than a rub.'

Angus knelt beside her, positioning himself so he could use his left hand.

'Here?' he said, pressing firmly into the area she'd indicated, wondering if she'd notice that his fingers were trembling. His right hand was resting on her hip, so close to the hardness of her stomach the slightest movement forward would allow him to feel the shape.

He concentrated on the task, moving his fingers to seek

out the little hollows near her spine, to press and probe and try to ease her pain.

'That's bliss!' she whispered. 'Just so great. Are you OK? Comfortable yourself?'

More comfortable than I've been for too long, he wanted to say, but he was uncomfortable as well, because added to the unexpected bliss of being close to her again was the physical stuff. Rationality told him he shouldn't find a pregnant woman sexy, but there was something so—voluptuous about her he found his body reacting every time he looked at her, let alone touched her.

So, although the sight of Stick performing these intimate duties for her was enough to make him squirm with jealousy, Angus realised it was probably safer that way.

Considering.

It was some time before he realised her breathing pattern had changed. She was asleep. He clambered stiffly to his feet and pulled one of the sheets off the couch, spreading it carefully over her, then studying her for a minute. Shining brown hair fell across her face, hiding all but the tip of her nose and her sensuous lips. He felt such a surge of love he wondered if he'd imagined the anger and recriminations they'd flung at each other, the cold distance they'd endured, before they'd agreed, with taut, sham civility, to go their separate ways.

He tiptoed away into the kitchen where he remembered there was no milk. He pulled open the refrigerator door, and stared into emptiness. There was also no butter, no eggs and no sign of anything substantial that could be cooked for dinner. Two rather tired-looking apples and a wilting lettuce seemed the sum total of Jen's fodder. He'd shop, that's what he'd do. Get some fresh bread rolls for lunch, perhaps some ham, and fish for dinner. Fish was good for pregnant women.

Back in the bedroom, he found his wallet and a scrap of paper so he could leave a note.

'Gone to the shops,' he wrote, remembering all the times he'd written similar explanations for his absence. Then he'd signed them with a declaration of his love and usually a silly face he'd drawn since they were both in high school. Well, she could have the silly face.

He walked briskly up the lane towards the shopping centre, waving to neighbours he knew by sight but not by name. The area had a floating population, few of the inhabitants of this beachside area permanents, but the check-out girl at the supermarket recognised him.

'Back in time for the baby to be born,' she said brightly. 'How was Africa?'

'Hot and dry, but interesting.' He answered the second question automatically, knowing she'd never understand his horror at the privations of the starving people he'd tried to help. But it was the woman's first question and its underlying assumption which nagged at him as he walked home. Their private life had always been just that, private, so only their closest friends had known of their problems with conception, of the eventual divorce. But was it right of Jen to let people assume the baby was his?

She was awake by the time he returned, sitting on the couch, folding and refolding his note between her fingers.

'You drew a face.'

'The check-out girl thinks the baby's mine.'

They spoke together so it sounded like a rather weird duet, but the uneasiness had been building as he walked back so he ignored her statement and added, 'Well?'

'I didn't tell her that,' Jen answered, and he knew she'd gone into defensive mode. 'After all, it's not the kind of conversation you have with chance acquaintances. I mean, I didn't advertise the divorce so naturally people will assume…'

She held out her hands in a helpless kind of gesture but he wasn't fooled. She was about as helpless as a lioness defending her cubs.

'How many *people*?' he demanded, dumping the shopping bags on the bench and coming closer so he could glare down at her. 'Patients? Staff? Friends?'

She shrugged and shook her hair back from her face.

'I don't know what the patients think,' she told him, 'but the staff all knew we'd separated, so did our friends—in fact, they're mostly the same people, aren't they? People like Jack and Nellie, Kathy and Mike—they're as much friends as fellow-workers. Even Neville, although he hasn't been in the practice very long…'

Angus stopped listening to what she was saying, seeking instead what wasn't being said. She was dodging away from the subject again, rambling on about friendship, trying to distract him. Well, it wouldn't work.

'Do *they* know it's not my baby?' he demanded, and saw a shadow of what looked like hurt in her eyes, and her chest rise as if she'd had to catch her breath.

'They know it was the result of a one-night stand,' she said, repeating the words she'd used earlier as if she knew their power to hurt him.

He stared at her, certain there was more to all of this yet angry again, unreasonably so—not so much at Jen, but at the unknown man. He walked back into the kitchen before he said something he'd regret. They'd know who was responsible, those friends and colleagues, and, come Monday, he'd find out.

What he'd do then, he wasn't certain, but surely the knowledge would make him feel better about all of this. He put the kettle on again—it was becoming a habit—

checked that she'd enjoy a ham roll for lunch, and set about fixing one for each of them, concentrating more than necessary on the task.

Jenessa levered herself off the couch and headed for the bedroom. She hadn't thought through the implications of Angus returning to work in the practice. She must speak to Jack while he was still at work. Explain what had happened and ask him to warn the staff to keep quiet about the baby.

With a cunning she hadn't known she possessed, she started the shower running first to mask the sound of her conversation, then she lifted the receiver off the bedroom extension and phoned through to the practice.

Betty, their relief receptionist, was on duty, and after the inevitable enquiry about Jen's health she put her through to Jack.

'But you wrote and told him,' Jack protested when he finally caught on to what she was asking. 'You wanted him to know!'

'I wrote and told him because all you busybodies up there insisted he had a right to know—that he should be told. Now he's home and he didn't get the letter so I don't want him to know.'

'Why on earth not?' Jack's yell almost pierced her eardrum.

'Because he doesn't want a baby, Jack. He never did. He admitted it before he went away and he's said as much again today. And even if he did…' Jen paused to sniff back a few maudlin tears. 'I don't want us to get together again because of the baby. If it were to happen, it should be because we love each other, not to give the child two parents.'

She held the phone a little further from her ear as Jack told her in no uncertain terms what he thought of both of them, which was in essence a lecture about two intelligent human beings behaving like children. In common with all their friends, he'd imagined the McLeod marriage had been one made in heaven, their divorce a small glitch which would soon right itself. Of course, he hadn't seen the destructive force of anger and frustration or felt the hurt they'd inflicted on each other in that final six months.

'So, you'll keep quiet about it?' Jenessa begged, when he'd exhausted his condemnation. 'And make sure the staff don't say anything.'

'I suppose so,' he grumbled. 'But you're wrong about this. I know Angus upset you, deciding to take off to Africa and save the world rather than staying here to at least try to save your marriage, but there's the baby's future at stake here as well.'

'I'm thinking of the baby,' Jen assured him. 'That's always been my primary consideration.'

'Well, be it on your own head,' Jack told her. 'And get it sorted out. You've only got, what, three weeks, before you're due?'

Jen listened to the click of the connection being broken and replaced the receiver.

'Be it on your own head.'

The words stayed with her as she stripped off her damp exercise clothes, dumped them in the laundry basket, then stepped under the shower. It echoed in her mind as the water rained down on her, splashing on the protrusion where a new life was entering the last phase of its antenatal development.

She wanted a warm, loving home environment for her baby, and her own experience had shown this was impossible in a marriage cobbled together for the sake of a child.

Her parents had been mature, intelligent people, both scientists working on university research projects. What miraculous eruption of passion had resulted in them making love Jenessa could never imagine but the discovery that her mother was pregnant had led to marriage. It had been a mistake for two such introspective people, totally self-absorbed, totally focussed on their own narrow worlds. The child they'd borne had grown up in a loveless and usually silent environment. From infancy she'd been placed by day in the child care centre at the university, at night cared for, bathed and fed by one or other of her parents, dutifully taking turns.

They'd done all the right things, of course, helping her with homework, even turning up for special occasions at school—when they remembered—yet it had been play-acting, for they'd remained polite strangers to each other and to her. It hadn't been until Jenessa had begun to visit other children's homes and had heard the squabbles and the laughter, seen the hugs and kisses, that she'd realised her world had been different.

And the seed of a dream that one day she would have a noisy, laughing, hugs-and-kisses kind of family had been planted.

Turning off water that had already run for too long, Jen stepped from the shower, dried herself, combed her damp hair, pulled on undies and another of the long, fitting dresses she preferred to wear at home, then sighed. Time to forget the dream and face reality.

CHAPTER FOUR

WHICH was lunch on the patio. How Angus had managed to set up the market umbrella with only one good arm Jen couldn't imagine, but it was there, providing a pool of welcome shade, and the comfortable folding canvas chairs had also been resurrected from the shed, two of them drawn up close to the table.

'The bed did prove too much,' Angus greeted her. 'I've admitted defeat and decided to wait until your friend returns from the footy. Now, I bought apple juice up the road, and I've also made tea. Which would you prefer?'

This was a switch! Angus at his most helpful and charming. Hadn't he been growling like a bear when she'd escaped to the bedroom? She stepped cautiously out the door onto the patio, not wanting to break the fragile truce.

'Tea would be lovely,' she said, settling into one of the chairs and looking down the long sweep of beach.

He returned with tea, poured her a cup, then waved his hand towards the spread he'd prepared. Fresh bread rolls already made up with ham, some biscuits he must have bought while he was out and a fruit bowl filled with fresh apples, pears and bananas.

'All major food groups covered to meet your nutritional needs, and the biscuits to satisfy a possible craving for sugar. Have you had cravings?'

He'd sat down beside her now, close enough to brush against if she moved unwarily.

Which she easily could do as this new caring and considerate Angus was making her uncomfortable. Not that he hadn't been both those things, and more, but today it was a ploy and although she couldn't read it she knew he was up to something.

'None at all,' she replied, aware two could play the nonchalance game. 'I guess that stage might have passed before I knew I was pregnant. I don't know if anyone's ever researched the timing of cravings.'

She reached out for a roll and began to eat, enjoying the bite of the mustard against the savoury taste of ham.

'Were you sick? No, I suppose not, if you weren't aware of your pregnancy. Throwing up every morning might have given you a clue.'

He smiled as he answered his own question, but the expression didn't reach his eyes. Close up, she could see the new lines pain had etched into his skin. She wanted to reach out and smooth at them.

'Before the knife attack, did you enjoy the work in Africa—? No, that's a stupid question—of course you wouldn't have enjoyed it. But was it what you expected?'

'Are you evading my conversation or genuinely interested?' This time the smile did reach his eyes, causing more problems than the indigestion from the mustard.

Jenessa dragged air into lungs cramped and starved of it by his expression.

'Come on, you know me better than that! Of course I'm interested.'

The smile became cooler, more enigmatic.

'Do I know you better than that, Jenessa? I'll admit I thought I did, but this?'

He touched her swollen belly very lightly, then drew back and closed his eyes. For a moment she thought he was going to continue on that line, asking again about the baby and its parentage, but when he spoke it was of Africa.

'You do what you can,' he said. 'At first, I didn't realise that simple truth, and was angry and frustrated by all I couldn't do—by the failures, the deaths that occurred no matter how hard we tried. But slowly I learned to concentrate on the positives. It's the only way to stay sane in an environment where a woman starves to death because she's giving her portion of the food ration to her child, then the following week the child dies anyway because supplies don't come through.'

'That bad?' Jen asked softly, and now she did smooth her hand down his cheek, her fingers damp with tears she'd wiped from her own eyes.

'Unbelievable,' he confirmed. 'I'll go back one day, but the people who said a two-year contract is too long were quite right. I think you do your best work for six months or maybe a year, while you're fresh and fit. After that, your own health will inevitably begin to break down, and familiarity with the suffering could isolate you from compassion.'

'Wouldn't that be good?'

He'd taken hold of her hand and she was content to let it lie in his, on his lap, warm against his skin.

'That's one theory, but I doubt it's the best. Organisations like Volunteers Abroad, which supplies teachers, engineers and health workers to isolated communities, use a two-year volunteer pattern, but emergency relief is different.'

Jen used her free hand to lift her cup of tea.

'That must be cold. I'll get you another,' Angus said, but she didn't want him to move, to let go of her hand, and stopped him with a quick denial.

'No, it's cool but very refreshing,' she assured him. 'Talk to me. Tell me more.'

And with her hand in his they sat on until the sun disappeared behind the house. His descriptions of the place and people were so vivid she could smell the dust and feel the heat. He told her of his fellow workers, the dedicated ones and the eccentrics, the strange jumble of humanity which had been thrown together in a tattered tent city on the edge of the desert.

'You're not sorry you went? In spite of your shoulder?'

'Not sorry because of that,' he said, 'but I often wondered if Jack had been right. If I should have stayed to see if we could make our marriage work again, instead of running away. He likened it to the melodrama of the old movies, with the hero running off to join the French Foreign Legion.'

Jen withdrew her hand. She'd known she could have stopped him, back then when he'd been making his arrangements to go. If she'd said, let's forget about babies, try again, give it another six months, he'd have stayed. But she'd been as stubborn as he had, and so bruised from all they'd been through that she'd looked forward to some time alone.

The slide back to the past had spoilt the mood between them. Could she lighten it again? Recapture it?

'He usually met a gorgeous woman, slung her over the saddle of his camel and rode off across the desert sand dunes with her,' she reminded him.

'Not this hero,' Angus said, 'although, unless I'm not mistaken, there's a fairly luscious specimen of womanhood heading over our dune right now. And me without my camel!'

Jen glanced towards the beach, saw their visitor and struggled out of her chair.

'Hi, Carole. Come on over. Would you like a cup of tea?'

Did she sound normal? Welcoming? She certainly hoped so, although what could only be jealousy was tangling the little tubes in her lungs so breathing was difficult, speech almost impossible. Normally, the sight of Carole's ultra-slim body did little more than provoke a determination to get back in shape as soon as she possibly could. Today, it was causing anguish.

'Oh, sorry. You two haven't met. Carole, this is Angus. Angus, Carole. Carole's Jason's sister, our other next-door neighbour.'

Having stumbled through the introductions, seen Angus rise very swiftly to his feet and hold out a hand in greeting, Jenessa headed back inside. She'd make fresh tea whether Carole wanted some or not. It would keep her out of hearing while Angus made neighbour jokes and ogled the lissom beauty.

Not that Jen could blame him for the ogling. She frequently ogled Carole herself, her eyes mesmerised by the young woman's perfect body, sculptured face and long golden hair.

Well, she couldn't hide in the kitchen for ever. She found a clean cup and saucer, and carried them, with the teapot, back outside.

'Actually, it's Jen who's done me the favour, keeping Stick out of mischief whenever I'm away,' Carole was saying when Jenessa returned. 'I'm a model, with assignments away from home a lot of the time, or working dreadful hours. He'd have been bored silly without Jen to fuss over, and because he feels responsibility towards her he's matured amazingly. I mean, what kid his age would actually volunteer to watch a birth? Yet he's looking forward to it tremendously. Every time I come home he's got some new and really gruesome bit of information about childbirth, and I know eventually I'll get the blow-by-blow description of the actual event.'

She turned to smile at Jen.

'I just hope you make it short and sweet. And definitely no operations. I'd pass out just listening to that stuff.'

She nodded affirmatively to tea when Jen held up the teapot, then swung her attention back to Angus.

'You're a doctor, too? Just back from somewhere? Stick says he knocked you out. Are you going to sue us?' She laughed merrily, throwing back her head so her hair shimmered like a golden waterfall, then she settled into the chair Jenessa had vacated and leaned towards Angus as he assured her he wouldn't hold the attack against her.

Jen poured tea and pushed the cup across the table towards Carole, reminding herself she had no right to be jealous and, anyway, flirting was second nature to the lovely model—it didn't mean a thing. But she was glad Angus would be starting work. Between assignments, Carole could be home for weeks.

Angus was talking about Africa now—not the medical stuff he'd shared with Jen, but telling funny stories about the people he'd met. Carole's eyes were wide with the wonder of it all, her lips slightly parted as if she were literally taking in every word he said.

'I'm going out to the shed to find the spare bed,' Jen announced, but no one seemed to hear her.

She walked around the house, instead of through it, realising just how close the house Carole rented was to hers—theirs. It hadn't ever bothered her before—in fact, she'd often been comforted to think if she yelled out in the night, Jason would hear her.

You can't be jealous, she told herself, but as she gazed down at her misshapen body and thought of Carole's slim loveliness, it was hard to stop the swamping wave of self-pity—an emotion so rare it was barely recognisable.

Angus finished his tale of a botched attempt to make their own water distillation plant, and looked around for Jenessa. He remembered her saying something but couldn't recall what.

'Do you remember where Jen went? What she was going to do?'

Carole seemed surprised by his question.

'Something about a bed?' she offered vaguely, her blue eyes looking deep into his, tempting him to stay, to make her laugh again. But he found himself anxious about Jen, wanting to look after her, as Stick did, to take responsibility for her. That's when he wasn't angry with her.

'A bed!' He leapt to his feet. 'No, she wouldn't be so stupid as to try to get it out herself. Come on.'

He grabbed Carole's hand and hauled her to her feet, dragging her behind him as he dashed around the house towards the shed.

Jen was sitting on the floor—in fact, she was sitting on a mattress on the floor.

'Are you all right?' he demanded, letting go of Carole to kneel beside his wife—ex-wife. 'You can't have been considering shifting this on your own, can you? Honestly, Jenessa, you are the most irresponsible woman!'

He ran his hands over her shoulders to assure himself she was OK, then down to touch the bulge, thinking of foetal heartbeats, not foetal movement, so when the kick came he was startled and then, as it was repeated, moved almost to tears.

'I felt it kick!' he whispered to Jen, then he grabbed her hand and pressed it to the spot. 'There.'

She turned to him and smiled, her face so close he fancied he could see the moisture of sadness in her beautiful eyes.

'I *have* felt it before,' she said gently. 'But it's always a thrill.'

His heart was thudding, his body aching with a need to kiss her. Not sexual need this time, just a hunger for a touch of her lips on his.

He stood up quickly and looked around for Carole.

'Hey, can you give me a hand with this bed?'

Better to be busy, to get on with practical stuff and stop thinking about Jenessa's lips and baby movements.

Carole seemed surprised, but she eventually realised he was serious, coming into the shed and obeying orders when he told her which end of the frame to carry.

'We'll be back for the mattress,' he told Jen. 'Don't you even think of moving it yourself. In fact, come inside and tell me where you want it.'

Would she unlock the spare bedroom or put the bed in the living room? It was strange, but now he'd felt that movement the baby had become real to him and he was curious to see the room Jen had prepared for it.

Would have prepared for their baby if things had been different!

'Where are you heading with this thing?' Carole demanded, dragging him out of his distracted thoughts in time to make the turn across the patio and in through the glass doors.

Jen had ducked in front of them and was shifting a small table out of the way. 'Here in the corner. With the front curtains drawn I won't get too much early morning light.'

He angled the bed in against the wall.

'I'll be sleeping out here, not you,' he told her. 'After all, I'm used to this bed.'

Carole looked from Jen to him, then back at Jen again.

'Hey, no arguing, you two—it's bad for the baby. Anyway, I came over for a free consultation.' She flashed her glorious smile. 'And look what I've scored. Two doctors for the price of one.'

'Consultation?' Angus was bemused, but it seemed Carole had sought free advice before for Jen simply smiled at her and waved her hand towards the couch.

'Sit down and tell us the problem,' she offered, then she followed Carole and settled opposite her in the chair. Which left Angus with the choice of sitting on the lounge beside the blonde beauty or—

He perched on the arm of Jen's chair.

'It's Botox,' Carole began, rubbing the tips of her fingers on the pale skin between her eyebrows.

'Botox?'

Angus was pleased Jenessa had echoed the word. It saved him showing his ignorance.

'The injection!' Carole said, as if that explained all. 'To stop frowning so I don't get frown lines.'

'Like a collagen injection?'

He hazarded a guess but it was evidently very wide of the mark for Carole gave a trill of laughter then explained, 'No, silly, it paralyses the muscles so you can't frown, and if you can't frown then you can't get frown lines.' She leaned forward and touched the corner of her left eye. 'You can have it at the corner of your eyes as well, but I stood in front of the mirror and tried smiling without my eyes crinkling up at all, and I looked peculiar so I thought I'd give that a miss for a while.'

She made it sound as if this decision was a serious and

major event, but Angus was still struggling with the first
part of the revelation.

'Paralyses the muscles so you can't frown?' he repeated, looking to Jenessa for help.

'I think I've heard of something similar being used in
general medicine to stop facial tics,' she explained.
'Seems now it's entered the beauty industry. I wish I'd
bottled it.'

'That's exactly what I wanted to talk to you about,'
Carole cut in. 'What is it? I asked the specialist before I
had it, and he assured me that it wasn't dangerous and
there'd be no side effects.'

She paused, then added, 'Well, he said I might get a
droopy eyelid but that would only last ten days and I had
a fortnight before my next assignment so I knew that
would be OK. And I stood up for four hours after I had
it—you can't lie down, you know—then Stick comes
home and says I'll get mad cow disease for sure. Does
it come from cows? Could I really get mad cow disease?'

Angus shook his head and looked down at Jenessa.

'She's all yours, Dr Blair. At least you seem to have
some inkling of what this is all about.'

Jen smiled up at him, merriment lurking in her dark
eyes.

'You're missing your big opportunity to impress,' she
murmured, then she turned her attention back to Carole.

'No, you certainly won't get mad cow disease, but I'll
look it up for you and let you know if there could be any
long-term or cumulative effects,' she promised.

'Cumulative effects?' Carole repeated.

'Something that happens if you continue to use it,'
Angus explained as Jen stood up and moved towards the
study. He'd forgotten they'd connected up their home
computer to the practice. She could get all the informa-

tion she wanted on the drug from on-line medical sources.

'Did you ask the doctor anything more about it? Why does Stick connect it with cows?'

If her brow muscles hadn't been paralysed, she'd have frowned, Angus decided, but, as it happened, her face remained totally unwrinkled although there was no doubt she was thinking about his question.

'I might have told him it came from cows, a long time ago when I first heard about it.'

A long time ago? She was what? Twenty-three?

And thinking about wrinkles?

He was about to ask her age when Jenessa returned.

'I thought I'd seen something recently,' she said, explaining her speedy information retrieval. 'It was in a medical journal but I'd skipped the article as it was aimed at dermatologists. It's made from botulinum toxin,' she said to Angus, then she smiled reassuringly at Carole. 'And there are no reports of adverse side effects, apart from droopy eyelids. But that doesn't mean there couldn't be long-term effects. It hasn't been in use for long enough to know, although the US Food and Drug Agency always carry out extensive tests before allowing human use of any drug.'

She sat on the couch beside Carole and looked into her face.

'You have great skin and you take good care of it, keeping out of the sun, drinking plenty of water. Did your specialist tell you it would only last four months?'

Carole nodded, smoothing at her brow again.

'I can have another then. He said sometimes after two or three it might last as long as eighteen months.'

'Or it might not,' Jenessa told her. 'In the article I read, the muscles eventually develop an immunity to it and it stops working altogether. If I were you, I'd give the injections a miss when this wears off and concentrate on facial exercises so the muscles keep your skin toned and firm. Then if you need the injection when you're older and your skin's less supple and resilient, it will still work for you.'

To Angus's surprise, this approach seemed to work for Carole, who leant across and kissed Jenessa on the cheek.

'Of course,' she said, smiles wreathing her face but not wrinkling her brow. 'That's a wonderful idea. You gave me those exercises once before. I'll go and hunt them out.'

She stood up and swanned gracefully towards the door, turning as she was about to walk out. 'If you need a hand with the mattress, Angus,' she said, 'give me a call.'

'Which reminds me,' Angus told Jenessa, 'of where we were before the botulism subject came up. I will sleep out here.'

'Nonsense. I get up and down all night to use the bathroom,' Jen said. 'So I might as well be out here.'

'I'm not taking your bed,' he argued.

'It's your bed too,' she reminded him, and again he sensed a sadness in her. Could it be she had as many regrets as he had? She'd made no move to stop him going away—in fact, it had been she who'd insisted on divorce. Yet…

'Let's get the mattress and argue about who sleeps where later,' Jen suggested, which began another argument as to which of them was least able to carry a mattress. 'Actually, it's purely academic for tonight as I won't be here. I mentioned the sleep clinic?'

Angus nodded, pleased she'd asked the question before he had time to demand whose bed she would be sharing. Besides, medical topics were safe neutral ground.

'Who's it aimed at? Insomniacs?'

Jen shook her head.

'Not this one. It's more for snorers and people who fall asleep during the day, monitoring them for incidences of sleep apnoea. The doctor who stood in for me last night was to do tonight's shift. I swapped, so it will be my turn tonight. Now, shall we get the mattress anyway?'

'If it's not wanted immediately, we can leave it where it is until your faithful retainer returns, either tonight or tomorrow some time,' Angus suggested. 'He and I will carry it.'

Jenessa grinned at him.

'That's probably a better idea than asking Carole to give you a hand. Until you insisted she help with the frame, I doubt she's picked up anything heavier than a jar of moisturiser for years.'

'Is that a catty comment, Jenessa mine?' he asked, using an endearment he hadn't offered her for a long time.

Her smile faded.

'I suppose it was,' she grouched, 'but she's just so thin and I'm so gross, she does tend to underline all the negatives of pregnancy.'

He took her hand and led her to the couch.

'You must be tired to even think that way,' he said, kneeling on the floor in front of her and reaching out so both hands touched her belly. 'You look more beautiful than ever—all aglow, Jen, truly radiant.'

'Oh, Angus!' she said, with a funny little catch in her voice that fired his pulse rate. 'Isn't this ridiculous?'

He didn't like the word at first, but when he considered his position and the sentiments he'd just voiced then 'ridiculous' just about covered it.

With more alacrity than grace, he stood up and settled

on a chair—too far away to keep on touching her no matter how much his hands might want to.

'Not as ridiculous as that child using some muscle-paralysing drug to stop getting frown marks. Is it really a derivative of botulism? I thought the stuff was deadly in the extreme—one whiff of it paralysing lungs—yet here are presumably ethical specialists pumping it into young women's facial muscles.'

'The derivation is true and apparently its use is widespread, but I'm not certain about the ethicality of using it on a woman as young as Carole. She's only twenty-five. Surely the specialist should have counselled her to wait, or offered less dramatic alternatives.'

'Well, you did that, and she appeared to listen. Will she take any notice, do you think?'

Jen sighed, then answered. 'She did once before when she was taking diuretics to lose some minute fraction of weight she imagined she'd put on. She's not anorexic or bulimic because she's too aware of the nutrition her body needs to keep exercising and working, but this was something new someone had mentioned.'

'And you convinced her to get off it?' Having seen Jen in action as she subtly persuaded Carole not to continue on Botox, he was keen to hear how she'd handled diuretics.

'I told her how they worked and said the excessive dehydration would dry her skin and cause premature wrinkles,' Jen explained, smiling now. 'She's really not as vain as that makes her sound, but her face and body are her fortune so she understands those kinds of arguments.'

'I can imagine!' Angus replied. 'Bulimia or not, she probably headed straight home and tried to throw up the tablets!'

Jenessa chuckled, a soft, comforting sound that made him realise how much he'd missed her company, and how right it seemed now he was back with her.

But he wasn't, was he?

And how did she see his return? Apart from the nuisance value of it?

The questions worried him enough to make him stand, and move away. He headed for the patio where he cleared away the remnants of their lunch.

By the time he returned, Jenessa was asleep again, curled up on the uncomfortable couch, breathing deeply and easily. He stacked the dishes in the sink, then returned to look at her, remembering the feel of the baby's movements against his fingers and wanting to touch her again. To hold his hand pressed against her belly, waiting for a movement.

Not on!

Afraid of waking her, he took himself out of the house. First he'd have a long walk up the beach, then come back and sort through the packing cases he'd left in the shed. If he was going back to work, he'd need some decent clothes. Hadn't they been insect- and vermin-proofed and stored out there somewhere?

Practical things, that's what he had to concentrate on. Forget all this physical and emotional stuff about Jenessa and the baby. After all, if she wanted a father for her baby, she'd have told the man who'd sired it. It wasn't his place to step into the role.

Or was it? What about wooing and winning? She was still Jenessa, wasn't she?

Could he step into the role of father?

Did he want to?

The questions chased him along the beach.

No revelations dropped like shining lights from the

sky, his mind going around and around as it tried to work out answers and failed, coming up, instead, with yet more questions.

He walked back, avoiding the house and heading straight for the shed. The mattress was gone! Clothes forgotten, he dashed across to the back door and barged in, his anger preceding him.

'If you shifted that mattress on your own, Jenessa, you're even sillier than I thought. A pregnant woman lumping things around—'

Jack Nielsen was sitting on one kitchen stool, Jenessa perched on another. In the far corner of the living room the bed was neatly made, a pile of clothes, which certainly weren't his, folded on a chair alongside it.

'Welcome home!'

Jack slid off the stool and offered his hand, but the smile on his face told Angus he'd made a fool of himself. Again.

'Hi, Jack, good to see you. I presume it was you who shifted the mattress, not the silly woman?'

Jack nodded, his smile fading as he added obscurely, 'But I agree with the "silly woman" tag.' He ran his professional gaze over Angus and continued, 'So, you're coming back to work with us for a while. It's good of you to agree to fill in. Jenessa tells me you've lost some movement in your right shoulder and arm, and that you're still in some pain. Do you want us to work out shorter hours? Jen's been cutting back on hers—when we could force her to—so it wouldn't take much rearranging of Neville's and my schedules to have you do, say, five-hour days.'

The words sounded OK, but there were puzzling nuances in the conversation. Or had Jack always spoken so formally?

'Five hours sounds great, but I could do more if I'm needed.' He responded to the words while trying to analyse his friend's manner—and the heartfelt agreement over Jen's behaviour. What was she up to that had upset Jack?

No time to wonder. Jack turned the conversation to Africa and the conditions there, to shop talk. Jen murmured an excuse and slipped away, disappearing into the bedroom and shutting the door. Was she accessing the bathroom from there, or packing more clothes so he could have the room and she the spare bed?

He answered Jack as best he could but his attention kept straying to that closed door—and the other one he couldn't see from here, the small spare bedroom which had once been his.

'Well, I'd better get going. Still on my way home from work. Nellie says she shows the kids photos of me every day so they'll remember what I look like,' Jack joked, but Angus got the impression the humour was forced, as the entire conversation had been. Jack wanted out of there as soon as possible, and, having done the polite thing and enquired about Angus's adventures, he was no longer obligated to stay. 'Say bye to Jen for me. She tells me she'll be working next week to help you settle in. No, no, stay there, don't see me out.'

Jack was blustering, Angus realised, as his erstwhile friend and colleague took off with more speed than grace. He'd been uncomfortable in Angus's presence, and couldn't wait to escape.

Why?

Angus glanced towards the closed bedroom door. Because Jack knew who had fathered Jenessa's child and didn't want to talk about it.

Angus followed him out the door, but he was too late.

Jack's car was already moving, heading up the lane at the maximum speed for safety in the restricted area.

He returned to the shed and found that the packing cases he'd left behind had also been moved. No doubt inside. No doubt by Jack. But acting under Jenessa's orders.

Well, he'd see about that.

CHAPTER FIVE

ANGUS stormed back into the house, and found his anger suddenly diffused, replaced by apprehension. The door to the spare bedroom was open. He took a cautious step forward and heard Jen's voice.

'You may as well come in—you'll see it some time.'

He took another uncertain step, his heart telling him he didn't want to see the room Jenessa had prepared for her baby, his head assuring him all baby rooms looked the same.

Well, maybe they did, but he knew he'd been in baby rooms before and none had ever made his heartbeat falter then race as if to catch up with itself.

The predominant colour was yellow, but such a deep, rich, golden version of the shade it made the word 'yellow' seem very ordinary. Bears appeared to be the theme, if rooms had themes. The curtains were patterned with cavorting bears while cut-outs of the lumbering animals, clad in blue, green and red overalls, hung from the ceiling.

'Nellie gave me the bassinet and I sewed a new cover for it, and the cot belongs to Kathy. She says she's keeping it for grandchildren so I'll give it back to her eventually. Jason found the rocking chair in that second-hand shop up the road and carried it all the way home. You can see why I had to shift the bed.'

'Yes, I can see why you had to shift the bed.' Angus spoke because he knew it was expected of him, but it was difficult, considering he was drowning in a swamp of emotions. This was so obviously Jenessa's vision, the room she must have prepared in her imagination so many times, only to have to shut the door on it each time a treatment failed.

He'd failed her also, comforting her, sure, but in his heart frustrated by her disappointment, not able to understand—until he saw this room—that every failure had been a death to her.

'Oh, Jen, it's beautiful,' he said, completing his survey of the soft toys stacked on a small chest of drawers, the change table and hanging sack of nappies. It seemed natural to reach out and take her in his arms, to draw her close—or as close as her obtrusion would allow. To nuzzle his face into her hair and smell the so-familiar shampoo, a Jen-smell he hadn't known he'd missed until this moment.

'I have to go to work,' she whispered. Husky-voiced with the emotion he was feeling?

'I know,' he murmured back, but still he held her, learning the feel of those new contours of her body against his, knowing he still loved her and wondering if love was enough.

Ships returning to harbour that was a tired old metaphor, Jen thought, but it was exactly how she felt. Or was she feeling this sense of homecoming because Angus's arms had always been her safe haven?

Until…

'Now!' she said, and slowly eased away from him. She looked up into his face and saw a confusion to equal her own in his gentle green eyes. Perhaps she should set aside her doubts, tell him the baby was his. Then he frowned and she shelved the idea, guessing the moment of closeness had been wiped away by some new aggravation.

'What's this nonsense about locking the room, about

break-ins? Stick said there'd been several. What happened?'

He sounded as if he held her personally responsible!

'There were three in all, beginning about six months ago—the first before I knew I was pregnant. That time, I came home late and went straight to bed. I didn't realise someone had been in until I got up next morning and saw the video player was missing.

'I phoned the police and looked more carefully then. My camera was taken, and the little radio we kept on top of the refrigerator, all small, easily carried stuff. I'd had the lap-top at work, so that was safe, but someone had been through the desk drawers, apparently looking for money. The police found the back door had been forced.'

'So you changed the locks?'

Jenessa turned away from him, carefully adjusting the row of bears on the small wardrobe.

'I was going to,' she assured him. 'I really was, but Jack was away at a conference, and we were flat out with an outbreak of food-poisoning which was eventually tracked down to a new food concession operating from a van at the beach—'

'So it happened again?'

Angus was growling at her now and she tried to shrug off his censorious attitude.

'But nothing was taken. I hadn't got around to filling in an insurance claim either. Apparently that's why they came back. The constable who came the second time explained that the young offenders who usually commit this kind of crime are canny enough to wait six weeks between visits. Generally speaking, this gives the householder time to replace the missing items. That way, the second time they break in, they score new goods.'

'And then you changed the locks,' Angus said, his voice edged with barely controlled patience.

'On the back door, but not the windows. The third time someone came in through the window and that was different. Whoever it was trashed the place, Angus, presumably angry because they couldn't find what they wanted.'

'Drugs?' He spoke quietly but the lack of volume didn't fool Jenessa for a minute.

'If they knew I was a doctor, it seems the obvious answer. I shifted in with Carole and Jason at that stage.' She hastened to placate him. 'Until I'd had specialists come in and work out how to make the place more secure. In fact, if you'd broken a window in an attempt to open it, the burglar alarm would have started and the entire neighbourhood would have turned out.'

It was silly, but memories of the dramas she'd been through made her want to snuggle back into Angus's arms. However, he didn't offer comfort and she knew she couldn't ask for it. Far better to get off to the hospital where her patients with sleeping problems would be arriving for another night of observation.

'I'd better go,' she said, and edged past him out of the room, pausing in the passage as she remembered her fears for the baby's room. 'Although I've got the place secure, I still lock this room and put the key into the bottom of the bathroom cabinet, in the cane basket with the cleaning rags.'

'Working on the theory that very few burglars would want to clean the bathroom while they're visiting.' Angus smiled as he made the silly joke but she sensed he was still upset. 'And you'd better show me how to set and unset the alarm or we might yet have all the neighbourhood turning out.'

'I'll get the spare keys for you. I've one for the back door and one for the alarm.'

Pleased to have something to do, she headed for the kitchen, where, following up on her theory about burglars and cleaning, she'd hidden the spare keys under the sink.

She showed him the small control box just inside the back door and told him the combination of numbers which would set it.

'How am I supposed to remember that?' he grumbled as she keyed in the numbers to demonstrate how it worked.

'It's our wedding date,' she muttered, twisting the key to shut it off then thrusting the keyring at him. 'I suppose that *will* make it difficult for you.'

She headed for the bathroom, and through it to the bedroom, where she grabbed a clean white coat and dragged it on over her clothes. Damn the man! One minute he was holding her in his arms and sniffing at her hair as if she were the most precious thing in the universe, and the next he was back to Angus the grouch.

Well, she'd lived with Angus the grouch for the last year of their marriage, and, while she was willing to admit he'd had cause to be grouchy—thrust into a demoralising process for a child he didn't want—she had no intention of blighting her life by forcing him back into a connubial relationship.

She packed a small bag, checked she had the car keys, then wondered what he'd do with himself for the evening. Although why she was worrying about him, considering his mood…

She walked back out to find him sitting on the lounge, leafing through the television guide.

'Can you drive with your shoulder? Would you like me to leave you the car? I can get a cab to the hospital.'

He glanced up at her and shook his head.

'If I stay awake long enough to watch the seven o'clock news I'll be doing well,' he admitted. 'I'm not sure if it's jet lag catching up with me or the effects of yesterday's adventures, but my shoulder's not the best so I'll fix myself something to eat then pop a couple of pills and hit the sack.'

'Some doctor I am!' Jenessa muttered, mentally chastising herself as she hurried towards him. 'I saw you taking tablets at lunchtime and didn't even think to ask if you were still in pain. How you could be so stupid as to shift that bed?'

'I used my left arm for the heavy stuff,' he assured her. 'And, in fact, the shoulder's not so bad. When Stick hit me yesterday, the blow, probably fortunately, glanced off my head and hit the wound area. That upset things a bit but not so much as to cause permanent damage.'

But Jenessa took no notice of his explanation, leaning over the back of the lounge and pushing the collar of his shirt to one side so she could assess the damage for herself.

The graft looked just as bad as it had the previous afternoon, and she ran her fingers along the raised ridge where the new skin had been attached. She shut away thoughts of what might have happened had the infection not been stopped, and carefully examined the scar.

'Actually, the graft must be taking quite well as there's a slight bruising from what I imagine is Jason's blow. For the skin to bruise, the blood supply must be getting to it. They've done a good job, those French surgeons.'

Angus said nothing, but she could feel tension radiating from his body so she set his collar straight and moved away.

'I'll be at the hospital if you need to get in touch.

They're co-operating in this clinic and have let us use the recovery rooms in the day surgery department.' She walked towards the back door, saw the alarm mechanism and wondered how she could ask him to stay safe without making him feel diminished by her concern. 'Angus, please, set the alarm when you go to bed. I know it sounds feeble but I always set it at night and now I've got this silly idea that if I once forget that will be the night someone tries to break in.'

She laughed to make light of her fears, adding, 'I mightn't have had cravings, but I guess I do have strange fancies.'

He stood up and came towards her.

'It's not a strange fancy after what you've been through,' he assured her—caring Angus back in place of the grouch. 'And I promise I'll set your alarm. I couldn't fight off a fit flea at the moment.'

He put his arm around her shoulders, in a casual gesture which was so familiar she knew it meant nothing, and walked with her, out of the house, around the shed, to the carport where they housed their little Mazda. He took the keys from her hand and unlocked the door for her, opening it and holding it while she wriggled her way into the ever-decreasing space between her belly and the steering-wheel. He handed her the end of the seat belt and watched as she positioned it carefully around her bulky body.

'Take care, Jen,' he said, then he leaned in and kissed her on the cheek. 'I'll see you tomorrow.'

She drove to the hospital with automatic ease, her mind churning with thoughts of Angus and the consequences of his return. But once there, she switched back to doctor mode, greeting the patients who'd turned up for another night of observation, chatting to them about their comfort, or lack of it, the previous night.

'It's all the tubes and wires,' Mr Parnell told her. 'I couldn't go to sleep properly with all those leads stuck to my body, so how can you tell if that's my normal pattern?'

'Tonight you'll be more used to them,' Jen assured him, 'and tomorrow night even more so. Eventually your normal sleep pattern will show up.'

'Eventually! After a month, I suppose, and we're only here three nights, you said.'

'It will show up within that time. It always does.' Katie Hynde, the nurse on duty with the sleep patients, was more bracing than Jen had been. She spoke with the authority of someone who'd been involved with the six-monthly clinics for some years. 'You wait and see. We don't have anyone who fails to graduate from this school.'

She bustled Mr Parnell into his room and Jen could hear her bullying him into his pyjamas. While Katie was settling him and the four other patients, and supervising their evening meals, Jen would have time to read some of the previous night's results.

Three of the men, Mr Parnell included, fitted the classic profile of sleep apnoea sufferers—middle-aged, overweight men. Mrs Gibson was also overweight but Jenessa felt there might be a physiological cause for her problem. The last patient, old Robert Williams, was more likely to be suffering from an age-related condition where during heavy sleep the brain sometimes failed to signal an impulse to breathe.

'You've got last night's sheets?'

Katie came in as Jen was spreading the print-outs on

her desk, the three men in one pile, the other two separate.

'Do you want to have a chat to any of them before we hook them up?'

'"Hook them up" being the literal description,' Jen said with a smile. 'Mr Parnell has already complained.'

Katie smiled at her.

'We always get one, but if you look at the graph that shows his different sleep states you'll see he slept best of them all on his first night.'

Jenessa pulled the sheet towards her and studied the lines drawn by the small machine, which acted on brain impulses transferred to it through electrodes attached to the patient's head. It showed his general sleep stages had been within the normal range but it also highlighted too many transient incidents when Mr Parnell would have woken to breathe although for such short instants he would not have been aware of them.

'OK, so I'll be sympathetic towards him but not too concerned about his grumbles,' she told Katie.

She left the papers on the desk and accompanied the nurse out of the small office they were using. Patients needed reassuring as the various probes and monitoring bands were attached to their bodies, and needed simple explanations of what went where and why.

'Where will we start?'

'Mrs Gibson. She's a love and never makes a fuss so we'll get into gear with her,' Katie responded. 'She's in here.'

Mrs Gibson greeted them with a broad smile.

'Lovely dinner. I should come to this hotel more often,' she joked.

She was sitting up in bed, and lifted one leg out from under the bedclothes.

'Ready to plug me in?'

Katie reached for the lead they would attach to Mrs Gibson's leg while Jenessa applied the gel which would make it adhere.

'Funny to think that how my legs move in the night can have anything to do with my sleeping,' Mrs Gibson said as Jenessa wrapped a band around Mrs Gibson's chest to monitor her chest movements during sleep and gauge the strain of breathing.

'I'll do your head now,' Katie said, attaching the electrodes with a swift efficiency, 'and Dr Blair will do the oximeter so we know how much oxygen is getting into your blood. There, you're almost done.' She looked up at Jen. 'What if you do the ECG and the sensors for the nasal and oral air flow and check everything's working, and I'll go on to Mr Stubbs.'

Jen finished wiring Mrs Gibson to the polygraph. There was only one channel left on the monitor. Should she use it for a microphone to record snoring? Many patients found this demeaning, and therefore more upsetting than all the wires. She'd check what Neville had used the previous evening and maybe set one up later.

It took two hours to get all patients uncomfortably bedded down for the night. Katie took herself off to the staff canteen, leaving Jen to sip at a glass of milk while she sat in the office, perusing the previous night's results.

Mrs Gibson's graph showed evidence of obstructive apnoea. Her chest had moved, indicating she was breathing, although there were regular occurrences of little or no upper airway flow. It indicated the airway was collapsing as the patient breathed in, restricting the passage of air to the lungs. In the early hours of the morning, when rapid eye movement sleep is most common, Mrs

Gibson's blood oxygen level had been very low and the ECG showed signs of some heart arrhythmia as a result.

If the pattern continued, she'd have to discuss the possibility of surgery, not a good option, or perhaps a positive pressure mask, although learning to sleep in such an uncomfortable device might be difficult. She was thinking through various alternatives when Katie returned.

'Mr Williams's graph is acting up.'

Acting up?

She followed the nurse to Mr Williams's room. The occurrence of ten apnoea episodes of ten seconds' duration in an hour was enough for a diagnosis but Mr Williams's apnoea was occurring far more often, the elderly man waking almost every minute.

'His blood pressure is too high to let it go on,' Jenessa said. 'We'll put him on a positive pressure mask for tonight.'

She wakened the patient and told him why, explaining that the mask was uncomfortable but that if he could get used to wearing it while he was being monitored then he could safely use it when he returned home. She showed him how the mask fitted and turned on the small blower which would provide the continuous positive pressure he needed to continue breathing during the night.

Would he be able to sleep?

'If he wants to stay alive, he'll learn,' Katie said, when she asked the question aloud a little later. 'Here's Mrs Gibson's chart. Dr Cantwell ordered thyroid tests for her yesterday.'

'Hypothyroidism. I wondered about that myself but she's new to the area and when I mentioned it to her she was adamant she'd been tested and was clear. Neville must have more winning ways with the women than I do.'

Katie grinned and blushed, as if Neville's winning ways had worked on her as well.

'You'd think most women who've put on a bit of weight would be glad of a physiological excuse like that,' she said.

'I know I would,' Jen replied, clutching at her excess weight and staggering across the corridor.

Katie chuckled and they went together into the next room, then checked each patient in turn, covering those who'd thrown off their light blanket, making sure the monitor print-outs weren't showing any problems that required immediate attention.

'Have a sleep,' Katie suggested when all had been carefully scrutinised. 'I'll wander in and out of the rooms and wake you if anything changes.'

'It's a welcome idea,' Jenessa admitted. 'Not that I need it. I've been as bad as these patients today, dropping into light catnaps whenever I sit down.'

'You're getting close to time and you work too hard,' Katie told her. 'You should have stopped work ages ago.'

'And done what?' Jen asked her. 'Sat around with my feet up?'

Katie chuckled. 'Yeah, I can just see you doing that.' She hesitated then said, 'Is it true Angus is back?'

Jenessa's heart sank. She should have gone and had a sleep and so avoided this conversation. But Neville would have had to explain her absence the previous evening. It was only natural he'd have mentioned Angus's return.

'Large as life and only slightly injured.'

Did that sound casual enough? And would the word 'injured' throw Katie off more personal questions?

'Injured?'

It worked!

Jenessa explained, in great detail, what had happened to Angus, spinning out the story until it was time to check the patients again.

'I'll go this time,' she offered, 'then maybe take you up on that offer and have a sleep.'

She hurried away. Katie had worked with them in the practice and, in Jenessa's opinion, had always been attracted to Angus.

Well, who wouldn't be? she thought gloomily as she watched Mr Gibson's chest rise and fall, pushed by the light pressure of the air now mechanically forcing its way into his lungs.

He was gorgeous, sexy and fun! Angus, not Mr Gibson.

She moved on to the next room, then the next, concentrating on medical matters to keep the *big* question at bay.

Which worked until she lay down on the bed provided for overnight staff and closed her eyes. An image of Angus's face as he'd seen her shape was printed on the back of her eyelids. She analysed it carefully. He'd been shocked but, more than that, he'd been horrified.

OK, so maybe that was because he had no idea it was his child she was carrying.

Should she have told him?

Probably.

So why hadn't she?

She felt the tears slide on to the pillow and let them fall, dampening the slip.

Stupid it might be—pathetic even in such a mature woman—but she wanted Angus to love her for herself. She wanted to know for certain that if they got back together again it was because he loved her, not because of the baby.

And what of the baby?

What if Angus loved her but the baby proved a barrier to that love?

She sniffed back the tears and breathed deeply, remembering the exercises, letting the air out slowly and ordering the tension from her body.

Katie woke her with a cup of tea and a selection of sandwiches from the canteen.

'OK, sleepyhead, rise and shine.'

Feeling drugged by her sleep, Jen eased herself into an upright position and squinted at her watch.

'Oh, Katie, it's four o'clock. You've let me sleep all night.'

'Four hours, that's all,' Katie corrected her, 'and you obviously needed it. Mr Parnell is an early riser so I thought I'd give you time to get properly conscious before he starts asking you questions.'

'Thanks!' Jen said, aware that the simple word did little to express the depth of her gratitude. And here she'd been thinking jealous thoughts about the night nurse.

She drank her tea, ate the snack and had a quick shower before facing Mr Parnell, who was adamant he hadn't slept a wink all night, then the other patients who reported various levels of satisfaction.

Mr Williams believed he could get used to the positive pressure machine and certainly looked a lot better than he had the previous evening.

When they were all awake, Jen arranged for them to have breakfast in a small staffroom. While they ate, she talked about the various remedies for controlling sleep apnoea.

'Weight loss is the single biggest factor in helping those with obstructive apnoea,' she explained. 'You don't fit that category, Mr Williams, but the rest of you do. A

positive pressure mask is the most effective way of en-
suring regular breathing during sleep until such time as
weight loss is achieved. They are uncomfortable devices
but Mr Williams managed on one last night, so if anyone
would like to try that we can hook you up to a machine
tonight.'

'Aren't there tablets we could take?' Mr Parnell asked.
'Surely that's the easiest way.'

It would be him, Jenessa thought, but she answered
carefully, trying to make him understand that the easiest
way wasn't always the best.

'Some forms of medication have been tried and have
worked with varying levels of success. It's not a permanent answer, like weight loss would be, but if any of
you would like to try medication, then we'll begin tonight
while you're still under test conditions. Apart from that,
there's surgery to remove some flesh from the back of
the throat and give your air intake a clearer passage. It's
not always successful and is an extreme option in any
case.' She smiled at them all. 'There, I bet that's confused
you enough for one day. Think about the various options
and tonight we can try whatever you think might work
for you.'

Mr Stubbs led the chorus of thanks, and one by one
they filtered out, leaving Jenessa on her own as Katie had
already gone off duty.

Sunday stretched before her, but not just any Sunday.
No, not with Angus back in the house, his mood swings
as erratic as her emotions. She wondered if anyone would
mind if she lay back down on the night-shift bed and
slept the day away.

She could even phone Bill Ramsay, who was the third
doctor involved in this weekend's tests, and tell him

she'd do his shift tonight. That way, she wouldn't have to face Angus again until work on Monday morning.

'And you'd be about as fit for that as a two-year-old!' she muttered to herself, and silently cursed the side effects of pregnancy, one of which was the amount of sleep she now required to function at anywhere near normal levels of efficiency.

She made her way slowly down to the car park and drove home, her heart jigging about at the prospect of seeing Angus again, her head telling her it was too late for them to fall in love again no matter how her heart behaved.

CHAPTER SIX

ANGUS wasn't there. A note, without the funny face, told her he'd gone shopping with Carole and Stick and didn't know when he'd be back. She was relieved and disappointed, contrary emotions she shut resolutely away, shoving them into a deep mental compartment with another intruder, jealousy.

What Angus did, and with whom, was his business, she told herself as she settled into her own bed and did a few breathing exercises to help her drift off to sleep. And, surely, with Jason along as well...

She dreamt of food, something rich and tantalising, a roast dinner. Angus in a frilly apron someone had once given her. In the dream, he was cooking roast lamb, his most renowned culinary skill, and she was thin again, her hair in a ponytail, perched on the bench between living room and kitchen, asking him about his sleep patterns while he peeled potatoes to put in beside the meat.

As she woke, the remnants of the dream remained, the smell of a succulent roast lingering in her nostrils. Could a smell remain in the memory so vividly it came back in dreams and stayed with her after she'd awoken?

The soft rattle of utensils in the kitchen told her it was more than a dream and unless there was a burglar who'd brought his own meat to cook in her oven then Angus was not only back, but preparing to feed her.

And possibly Carole and Jason.

The postscript to her thought dimmed her anticipation slightly, but not enough to stop her slipping quietly out of bed and heading for the bathroom. A treat like this required special preparation for the guest as well. So far, since his return, Angus had seen her tired and harassed after a day at work, rumpled and grumpy after sleeping on the couch, and sweaty from her exercise.

He'd said she was beautiful, but that had been to soothe her pique at Carole's slimness, but she could look OK if she made the effort. Shower first, then body lotion. The thought of stretch marks didn't bother her, but she felt better after she'd smoothed the fragrant moisturiser into her skin.

And the red dress.

Earlier in her pregnancy, when she'd bought it to attend a friend's wedding, it had clung to her increasing figure quite modestly, but now it stretched almost brazenly around her curves, and revealed the deep cleft between her burgeoning breasts. She looked at her reflection in the mirror and wondered. She certainly wouldn't have worn it outside the house, but for lunch with Angus?

Well, if she wanted to look her best this was it.

And she did want to look her best, although she daren't pursue the 'why' of that desire.

She spread a different moisturiser on her face, added a filmy make-up base which smoothed out the increasing brownness of her skin, a touch of blush to suggest a healthy glow and dark liner around her eyes.

He hair hung around her face, making her look more like a pregnant schoolgirl than the sophisticate she was trying to project. She scooped it up and held it on the top of her head with a big red plastic butterfly clip. Casual enough for Sunday lunch but the style made the bones in her face look more prominent.

Mascara and lipstick completed her preparations—well, almost. With a smile teasing at her lips, she dug through the clutter in the bathroom cabinet, searching for the half-empty bottle of perfume Angus had given her.

He'd been walking through the perfume department at the local department store one day, heading innocently towards the lifts. A saleswoman had been passing out samples of a new product, spraying a little of the rich liquid onto small squares of blotting paper and handing them to passersby. Angus had been hooked, paying out as much money as he'd spend on several new shirts for a large bottle of Calvin Klein's Eternity.

She dabbed a drop behind each ear, on her wrists and the insides of her elbows, then wet her finger with it and slid it down between her breasts.

'Lunch in half an hour,' Angus called. 'Do you want a drink beforehand? A glass of wine perhaps?'

Hell, why not?

'Half wine, half soda, thanks,' she called back, checking her appearance once again before leaving the bathroom. As she crossed the bedroom, nerves threatened to overcome her. Wasn't she overdoing things for a simple Sunday roast? Should she pull off the dress and put on jeans and a baggy shirt? Or perhaps her all-concealing overalls?

'Drink's poured.'

Angus's voice put an end to her dithering. She slid her feet into flat sandals, took a steadying breath, and walked casually out of the bedroom and into the kitchen as if she dressed for lunch every Sunday.

He turned at the sound of her footsteps, and the only hint of his reaction was the way the wineglass he was holding trembled slightly so the liquid slopped down over his fingers.

'I thought I was dreaming when I smelt it,' she said,

settling on one of the kitchen stools and taking the glass from his hand. 'This mine?'

His mouth opened but no words came out. It closed again and the glazed expression began to fade from his eyes, to be replaced by what looked like a quick flare of anger.

'I hope you don't go out in public dressed like that!' he growled, but she realised there was more than anger building. In her it was desire, as irrational as her decision to dress up, but was it a similar desire or something else drawing Angus towards her, almost imperceptibly, like a child moving reluctantly to answer a parental call?

When he was close enough for her to see his chest expand as he breathed in her perfume, he reached out and touched her. Lightly on the shoulder at first, then sliding his hand down towards her breasts, lingering for a fraction of a second before it moved upwards again, following the line of her neck, upwards until his knuckles brushed across her cheek and pressed against her lips.

'Are all pregnant women as sexy as you? Is this something I've been missing in my study of the opposite sex?' His voice was hoarse, as if the strain of breathing had tightened his vocal cords. 'Hell, Jenessa, if you knew the effect you're having on me…'

She could see the effect, in fact, and was more than a little concerned to find it was mutual. She'd wanted to knock him out, but had foolishly imagined remaining cool and calm herself.

'It's chemical,' she said, as lightly as the circumstances allowed. 'Our hormonal signals getting reacquainted.'

'Oh!' he said softly, bending towards her, his gaze steady on her eyes, holding her captive. 'Is that all?'

His mouth brushed softly across hers, blanking out her mind with sensual, not visual, memories, so her lips responded, seeking more of his, clinging at first then doing their own exploratory foray. They opened as his tongue touched them and the taste of him was so familiar yet so new she felt the heat rush through her body, surging upwards to warm her cheeks, downwards to tease and moisten her most private parts.

Angus held her shoulder, to steady himself, he'd thought, when his brain had still been working. As the kiss deepened he could feel a trembling through that hand but couldn't tell which of them was shaking or, if both, who was the worse.

His body raged with a need as hot as fever, wanting to take her, here in the kitchen, on the bench, the floor, a chair, wherever! And however, given her condition! But he couldn't release her lips, couldn't tear his mouth away from the feel of them, the delicious wetness of her mouth, responding to him as hungrily as his was demanding.

'Something burning in there?'

Stick's voice brought Angus jerking upright so swiftly he cricked his neck and yelped at the discomfort. Jen's lips were full and pink, her cheeks flushed a hectic red to match her dress, tendrils of hair falling about her face, giving her an abandoned, wanton look.

'Come in,' he managed to say, moving to stand between Jenessa and the doorway and adding to her, over his shoulder, 'I forgot to tell you I'd asked Stick and Carole to come over for lunch.'

At the time it had seemed like a good idea, to save him being alone with Jen for the afternoon, but now?

Now more than ever, he told himself, then thanked Carole as he took the bottle of wine she was offering and waved the visitors towards the dining table which stood on a rectangular rug at one end of the big living room. Behind him he heard a slither of material as Jen slid off her stool and then the sound of her footsteps beating a quick retreat.

'Hi, you two. I'll be back in a sec.' She threw the greeting at the visitors then shut the bedroom door, and, true to her word, was not long returning. Her hair was still caught up on the top of her head, held by some gravity-defying clasp, but it was tidy again, not wantonly abandoned at all. She'd also pulled on a loose cotton shirt which hid the brazen outline of her shape but did nothing to conceal the seductive fullness of her breasts.

If anything, she looked sexier.

He refused her offer of help, waving her towards the table with the others, saying he'd prefer to have the kitchen to himself, which—given the circumstances— was true.

As far as he could judge, the lunch went well, the conversation moving easily from one topic to the next. He felt divided, on one plane his corporeal body playing host, while on another his mind threw up unlikely fantasies and tried to recall what he'd learned about sex and pregnant women. OK in the beginning, he knew that much, but in the last trimester? It made him wonder just how pregnant his ex-wife was, and why he hadn't thought to ask.

Then, in the way things had been happening since his return to this house, the unasked question was answered when Carole said, 'So, Jen, three weeks to go. Looking forward to the big event?'

As Jenessa answered, Angus did the sums. Three from forty leaves thirty-seven weeks, roughly eight months, given the extra days in each month, back to her last menses. The numbers fell into place and he stood up, muttered an excuse about seeing to something in the kitchen and walked away from the table.

Bad excuse! The kitchen offered no concealment and right now he needed privacy—preferably somewhere he could hold his head in his hands and howl, giving vent to his disbelief that Jenessa could have gone straight from him, and their glorious lovemaking that night before he'd left the country, to some other man. He made for the bathroom, but didn't howl, slumping instead onto the toilet seat and wondering if he wanted to be sick.

Or perhaps murder her in a fit of jealous rage.

He splashed his face with cold water instead, then flushed the loo to give him an excuse for the disappearing act. He walked back out to the kitchen and clattered about, making more noise than necessary to cut an ice-cream dessert and arrange the slices in the small crystal bowls which had been a wedding present from an aunt.

Stick was clearing away the dinner plates while Carole and Jenessa were apparently discussing men. From where he stood, it sounded as if Carole was asking Jen's advice and he was tempted to make scoffing noises.

Not that they'd recognise his reaction as disbelief, or understand its cause, he decided.

Stick put the plates in the sink and ran water over them before stacking them neatly in the dishwasher. And that was another irritation, Angus realised. The kid's familiarity with this house—Angus's house. Though which half of the dishwasher was his, he couldn't say!

He pushed the dessert dishes across the bench, then walked around and passed them to the table from the other side. As he leaned across Jen's shoulder to put hers on the table in front of her, his arm brushed against her and she lifted her hand and touched his wrist in a kind of silent thank-you.

Or perhaps a reminder of where they'd been when the visitors arrived?

'Well, you're no help at all,' Carole was complaining to Jenessa. 'Having always been a one-man woman, you've got no idea of the hassles of having to choose.' She turned a glowing smile on Angus. 'Perhaps I'd better go for a male opinion. Which should I choose? The lawyer or the architect?'

'Is this for a permanent arrangement?' Angus asked, bemused by the question but pleased to find an escape from his thoughts.

Carole's laugh rang through the room. 'No, silly,' she protested. 'For a date in Cairns next Wednesday night. I was up there last month, doing a promotion at the casino, and they've asked me to come back for another shoot. The lawyer's dark and we probably look better together, with me being fair. I think that's important, don't you?'

If he'd been bemused earlier, he was staggered now. Surely she wasn't serious. He turned to Jen and caught a glimpse of the teasing laughter in her eyes before she swung to face Carole and applied herself to the question with a straight face and a tone of voice oozing sincerity.

While he and Stick ate ice cream, and he, at least, pretended the conversation wasn't happening, the two women coolly and dispassionately dissected both candidates for Carole's attention, settling, in spite of the colour clash, on the blond architect.

'Is that how you chose the baby's father?' Angus demanded when the visitors had departed and the cause of all his angst was lying on the couch with her head on one rolled arm and her feet propped on the other. Her hands were crossed contentedly across her belly. 'Added up his physical characteristics like a newborn's Agpar score?'

She turned her head so she could see him over the back of the couch.

'Oh no,' she retorted. 'I gave marks for intelligence as well. I then considered staying power and work ethics but decided those might be environmental rather than genetic characteristics.'

He knew she was teasing, as if she'd guessed his mood and was trying to lighten it, but he didn't want lightness at the moment. He wanted answers, and possibly revenge.

A shrill summons from the phone spoilt his plans for either. He lifted the receiver on the kitchen extension and growled a hello. Someone for Jenessa, a Mr Parnell.

He took her place on the couch and listened to her end of the conversation.

'Yes, Mr Parnell, it is uncomfortable.'

'No, Mr Parnell, of course you don't have to continue. It's entirely up to you.'

'No, I do understand.'

'Well, if you decide to see someone else at a later date, I'd be happy to pass on the data we've already collected.'

There was no goodbye so the man must have hung up before she could do the polite thing.

'Drop-out from your sleep clinic?' he asked, as Jenessa walked back and sat down opposite him.

She shrugged her shoulders and said, 'It's no skin off my nose, but I'm sorry he's done it.' She studied Angus for a moment, as if trying to decide if she should share whatever concern was eating at her. Then she gave a little nod as if the decision had been reached.

'It's the thought of having to lose weight that's bothering him,' she continued. 'He hasn't said so but I'm sure that's what it is. Do you think we've been doing the right thing, stressing the weight loss before participants have spent three nights with us?'

It was a strange question—strange subject, come to that. Sleep apnoea could cause a deterioration in a person's quality of life, but there was only anecdotal evidence to suggest it might cause death through heart arrhythmia. Yet Jen seemed genuinely concerned about this patient's defection, as well as the programme itself.

Or was she simply sticking to safe medical conversations to avoid their talk becoming personal?

Not such a bad idea, given what had happened earlier—and how he'd felt when he'd done his mental arithmetic! He went with the safe medical matters and answered her.

'Weight loss is the first thing to try so the sooner the patient realises that will probably cure him or her, the better. You know how information dissemination works. You give people a lot of information and they absorb some of it, but retain more if they can come back and ask questions. If you leave mention of weight loss to the last morning of the clinic, patients don't have the opportunity to get back to you about it unless they return in a regular appointment time. Are you offering weight loss assistance?'

She leaned forward in the chair before she replied.

'Yes. They were each given a diet sheet this morning, and we're offering weekly weigh-ins and group support meetings at the surgery. Katie Hynde has been on duty during the clinic and she'll conduct the weekly meetings and do follow-up with the attendees' partners to see if it's made a significant difference.'

Angus heard the words but he was more concerned about her actions and the way her voice had trailed off towards the end of her explanation. She was rubbing at her back and her face was pale.

'You OK?' he asked, as the implications of back-rubbing made his heart race.

'I will be in a minute. It must have been the bed I slept

in at the hospital—I've been having back pain on and off all day.'

Dear heaven, could it be the beginning of labour? He couldn't cope with this! Wanted to be back in Paris. In Africa. Anywhere but here.

Told himself to remain calm and actually listened to that inner voice, rising out of the chair in a relatively normal manner instead of a panic-stricken leap to his feet.

'Why don't you lie down on the bed and let me rub it.' He put out his hand and helped her to her feet. 'No, on your own bed, not that one,' he insisted as she headed for the corner of the living room.

She didn't argue, which made him realise how bad the pain must be, so he put his arm around her shoulders and walked with her, trying to take her weight, thinking how precious she was to him and how he couldn't bear it if anything were to happen to her.

Which was a mind-boggling concept, given his earlier anger and the present circumstances.

Jen pulled off her shirt then lay on the bed, curled inwards, and again her hand guided him to where the pain was greatest. He sat behind her and kneaded at her spine, then saw, through the fine material of her dress, the unmistakable movement of a contraction.

Forgetting all doctorly advice about staying calm and keeping the patient from panicking, he said, 'Jen, that's a contraction—you're in labour. What do I do? Who do I phone? Are you timing them or should I?'

He glanced at his watch but his mind failed to register the time. He stopped back-rubbing to put both hands on her belly, and was startled when he felt it move again.

'They're too close. We have to get you to the hospital. Who's your doctor? Did you tell me? Jen, don't just lie there!'

Could she hear the hysteria in his voice or was it only in his own ears he sounded demented?

Apparently not, for she was laughing at him, and the movement he could feel was caused by her glee.

'Ever hear of a guy named Braxton Hicks?' she asked.

'Braxton Hicks?' It rang a bell. Was he her doctor?

'Braxton-Hicks contractions.' She stopped laughing for long enough to explain. 'I've had beauties. Right from the first trimester, but getting stronger and more regular as the pregnancy progressed. I tell myself it's good practice for the muscles when the real thing begins but that doesn't stop them being painful.'

Braxton-Hicks contractions! What an idiot he'd been not to think of that! Or was he? Hadn't he learned where they could be mistaken for the real thing—no, that the real thing could be mistaken for Braxton-Hicks?

'Are you sure that's all they are?' he demanded. 'This late in your term, couldn't they just as easily be the beginning of labour?'

She curled into a tighter ball and he realised she was suffering another wave of strong pain.

'I don't think so,' she replied, breathing deeply then blowing the air out through her mouth. 'I'll have a series of them then they'll fade away, you'll see.'

He continued his back-rubbing, but his fingers worked mechanically, his mind dredging through years and years of accumulated learning, seeking out whatever information he may have retained about late pregnancy and labour.

Odd and totally useless snippets came back to him. There was also a Braxton-Hicks version of the movements used to turn a foetus from a bad position. And old Braxton Hicks, for whom the contractions and the movement had been named, had been called John.

'Effleurage!' The word popped out as suddenly as it had appeared in his head.

'I beg your pardon?'

'Effleurage—that rubbing business on your tummy. It's good for Braxton-Hicks contractions. I can see the picture in the textbook as clearly as if I read it yesterday. Here, sit up a bit and lean back on these pillows and I'll give it a go.'

Feeling more confident now he had something to do, he helped her into a half sitting, half lying position on the bed and began to massage her stomach, feeling the shape of the foetus, well positioned with its head tucked low and its little butt pressing high against Jenessa's diaphragm.

He could feel her breath on his cheek as he leaned over her so his hands could follow a circular pattern, and he sensed she was relaxing while he was becoming more and more tense. Wooing and winning—what a laugh!

'I still love you, Jen,' he said, keeping his eyes on the red material so he didn't have to see her reaction to the words.

'It's a strange time to be telling me that,' she said lightly.

'It's a strange situation,' he replied, his hands still moving round and round and round.

'Is it?' she asked. 'Wouldn't this have been normal if it had happened early in our marriage, or even then did you not want a child?'

He stopped the gentle massage and turned to look at her, to meet her dark eyes and see the questions repeated in them.

'I don't know,' he replied, as honestly as he was able. 'I suppose, if it had happened, I'd have had time to get used to the idea of—'

Stopped dead as he suddenly remembered a day when he'd decided he didn't want to have a child. He'd been sitting in on a postnatal clinic and a woman who'd looked a little like Jen had been one of the patients. She'd had the six-week-old infant in her arms, and a toddler of about two clinging to her skirt, whining constantly about some long-forgotten need. He'd seen the dark circles under the woman's eyes, heard the brusqueness in her husband's voice as he'd chastised the child and tried to remove him from the mother's side.

They had looked to him like a family coming apart at the seams—at a time when they should have been rejoicing in the birth of the new baby.

Could he explain this to Jen? Would she understand? Perhaps not all of it, but he'd have to try.

'I think it was partly my own upbringing, plus a wedge of immaturity, and a measure of jealousy as well. I didn't want to share you with anyone. I'd done enough medicine to know how dependent children were on their mothers, seen couples grow apart during those early days of child-rearing.'

'Some couples are drawn together,' Jen pointed out, and he grinned at her.

'I do know that—I just couldn't see it that way.'

She sighed.

'Then why go along with the IVF in the first place? Why didn't you say something right at the beginning, instead of doing the martyr thing—going ahead with the tests and treatments as if our marriage had a scoresheet and you were amassing Brownie points.'

Good question. Again he had to think back, to try to recall his emotions at that time. They'd been married six years and Jen had been off all contraception for twelve months. Bingo! It was the contraception argument. He let his hand rest on her full belly, let his fingers stroke it gently as if to atone for all that had happened in the past.

'I felt guilty,' he admitted. 'Remember the arguments we'd had, even before we were married, about you going on the Pill. You said I should take some responsibility for contraception, suggested we take turns—you for six months, then me for six months. I argued convenience—that we were both on duty at different times and meeting up at different places, so what if we found some time together and I didn't have a condom?

'My point was that it was safer, surer protection but that wasn't the whole story. I did try wearing condoms a few times, but I hated it so I pushed for you to take the Pill.'

She straightened to a sitting position as if she needed to be upright to consider her answer.

'You felt guilty? After all this time, you now tell me you felt guilty about letting me take all the responsibility. You never showed marked signs of guilt back then!'

She was flushed, presumably with anger, and looked so beautiful he had to touch her heated cheek.

'Well, I didn't feel guilty while you were on the Pill because to me it seemed such a simple thing for you to be doing. Now, too late, of course, I realise that as well as being pathetically immature I was also entirely selfish.' He reached up and took the clip out of her hair so the strands could tumble free. 'But when you went off it, and failed to fall pregnant, I began to wonder if it might have been because of the length of time you'd fooled your system into not ovulating. Of course I felt guilty.'

She ran her fingers through her hair then tried to smooth it into place.

'But the Pill had been on the market for years by the time I started it, and tried and tested so many ways. I'm sure I've read that difficulty in falling pregnant has been ruled out as a long-term effect of oral contraception.'

'I knew that. It was one of the arguments I'd used to get you to take it,' he admitted, taking her hand and holding it in his. 'But later on the knowledge didn't stop me wondering. Or feeling bad about it. Perhaps, by then, I was actually beginning to grow up.'

This time she stroked his cheek.

'You were grown up enough for me, but I can't believe you went through all of that because of guilt,' she said softly.

'And love,' he added. 'I knew how much it meant to you. I did want it to happen for your sake, Jen.'

'Which brings us back to where this conversation started,' she said, moving away from him now, edging off the bed and standing up as if his answer might be better dealt with from a distance. 'You may still love me, but I'm about to have a child. I'm a "two for the price of one" package these days, Angus.'

'Love me, love my child?' he asked, while his heart faltered, wondering if that was possible. She didn't answer but walked away into the bathroom, leaving him with more than that unanswered question.

Could he love this child she was carrying, no matter who had fathered it?

Love it as he would love a child he had fathered?

But would he love a child he'd fathered? Wasn't that the ultimate question, the source of all his doubts?

Her doubts?

CHAPTER SEVEN

JENESSA brushed her hair and told herself that Angus's declaration of love didn't mean he wanted them to get back together again.

It's what you wanted, her heart argued. For him to love you for yourself, not the baby.

He has to love the baby as well, the sensible voice replied.

But you're making it too hard for him, by not telling him he fathered it. You're being silly.

She flinched as another contraction grabbed at her, breathed deeply then sighed as she exhaled. Her head knew what her heart was saying, but it persisted in its warning for her to hold back. Was it pique because he'd forgotten that last night they'd spent together? Or anger because he'd assumed she'd go from him to another man?

She put the brush away in the cabinet and sighed again. She'd have a shower, which would give Angus time to vacate the bedroom and find something to do somewhere else. Then, clad in more sensible clothes than a clinging red dress, she'd go up to the hospital in time to greet the sleep-clinic patients. Bill Ramsay was on duty tonight, but she could talk to him about Mr Parnell, grab a meal up there, and by the time she returned plead tiredness and go to bed.

It would be a temporary escape, nothing more, but wasn't there a saying about tomorrow being another day? She'd handle it when it arrived.

Wrapped in a voluminous towel, she emerged from the bathroom to find her first assumption had been wrong. Angus hadn't found something else to do elsewhere. In fact, he was right where she'd left him—on the bed. Only this time he was asleep.

She crept closer, drawn by the opportunity to study him more closely. The loss of weight he'd suffered had made the bones stand out in his face, giving him a tougher, more mature appearance.

Did it go deeper than appearances—that maturity?

Had he been so immature?

She turned away, dressed quietly and wrote a note for Angus. She thought about maturity—her own as well as his—as she drove to the hospital.

'What were you like as a student and young doctor?' she asked Bill as they ate together after all the patients had been settled.

'Hopelessly immature,' he replied so promptly she wondered if her mental processes had cued him.

'Do you mean as a doctor? Medically immature? That scary "first time doing it all by yourself" feeling?'

He shook his head.

'Oh, no, although I'll never forget that sick feeling the first time I gave an IV injection, the first time I slit the patient's skin for an appendectomy, the first time I sutured a wound. Wasn't it hell? You'd seen it hundreds of times, yet to do it yourself…

'Horrible,' she agreed, 'but we all go through that. What did you mean by immature if it wasn't work-related?'

He shrugged, as if regretting he'd made the statement now she was persisting.

'I don't think it's the same for women who study medicine. I've always suspected females are far tougher than we men, but for a male student it's as if you're shielded from the real world for a long time. First at school and because you have to be bright to get into the course, you get preferential treatment there, then the university years where, generally speaking, you do two things, studying and partying, and again you don't get much of a view of real life.

'So you land in a hospital as an intern and, although all ward sisters know more about medicine than you'll probably ever learn, they kind of defer to you. Yes, Doctor, no, Doctor. It's not hard to think you're something special.'

'Something special.' Jen repeated the words in her head. The only person who'd ever made her feel that way was Angus.

'Did ward sisters really toady to you in that way?' she demanded. 'All they ever made me feel was terrified.'

Bill smiled.

'I told you it was different for women doctors. It's a known fact that girls mature younger than boys, so most of the women who go into medicine are already, emotionally, years ahead of their male counterparts. You probably didn't read the ''yes, Doctor, no, Doctor'' as obeisance but as normal agreement. I'm just telling it the way it seemed to me. I felt I was two people—the visible doctor whom everyone respected as a fount of wisdom and knowledge, and the real me who knew nothing and was terrified of being found out.'

'Well, we had that in common,' Jen agreed. 'I think we all had that uncertainty beneath the overwhelming tiredness of those first years.'

The talk drifted to other things, but some of Bill's explanation stayed with her and she said goodbye and headed for home, determined to have a sensible conversation with Angus and perhaps tell him...

She couldn't tell him much when he wasn't there. All his talk of still loving her hadn't stopped him going to the movies with Carole. Jen showered again and set up a lamp by the bed in the living room, thinking she'd read for a while before she went to sleep.

A slight noise filtered into her consciousness, rousing her enough to be confused about where she was. She lay in the darkness, trying to remember, then gradually made out the perimeters of the room, the shape of furniture. Angus must have turned out the light. Perhaps that's what she'd heard.

She sat up and peered towards the bedroom, hoping to see a line of light beneath the closed door, but if Angus was home he must have been sleeping. Easing herself off the bed, she stood up, took one step towards the hallway and heard the fierce shrieking, clanging, indescribable clangour of the alarm. The racket hammered in her head, making her slump back on the bed and clasp her hands over her ears. Then lights came on, the noise stopped and Angus was by her side, his arms around her, holding her trembling body close to his and making soothing noises.

'Jen, are you OK?' The noises became decipherable. 'I imagine whoever set off the alarm has long gone but I should check the other rooms just in case.'

She felt him move and clung to him, as desperate as a drowning child, needing to lean on his strength while she recovered.

'It's stupid to go looking for intruders—dangerous stupidity,' she managed to tell him. 'Anyway, it wasn't an intruder, it was me.'

'You?'

He still held her but shifted slightly so he could see

her face, and as he waited for her explanation his fingers brushed her hair back from her face, and one gentle thumb wiped the tears from beneath her eyes. She snuggled against the arm that held her close, trying to halt the tremors still chasing through her body.

'It's the alarm. There are alarms on the windows, but in case the power is cut off there are battery-operated electronic sensors in this room. I forgot to tell you not to walk out here once the alarm is set. I didn't think about it myself when I made up the bed.'

He hugged her close.

'So, my doing the right thing and setting the alarm caused all this fuss?' he teased, then, as if her trembling had transmitted itself to his skin, he helped her gently to her feet. 'Come on, I'll put you back to bed where you belong.'

She went with him into the bedroom, excused herself for the inevitable bathroom stop, took time to wash her face and brush her hair, then walked back into the bedroom where Angus had straightened his side of the bed and was picking up a book from the bedside table.

The shaking began again.

'Stay with me?' she asked—no, not asked, more like pleaded.

He seemed to stiffen as he turned to face her, his eyes hooded, his expression unreadable.

'Are you sure?' he asked, and she tried to answer but found her throat choked with emotion, so she nodded in reply and sank down on the edge of the bed, manoeuvring her way between the sheets and turning on her side into the only position she found comfortable for sleeping.

Then the light went out and Angus was beside her, his body curled around hers so her back pressed against him. His hand rested lightly on her hip—where it belonged.

It's your baby, she wanted to say. In fact, she imagined she could hear the words permeating the darkness.

Not yet, caution whispered, so she pretended she wasn't deliriously happy to be in bed with Angus again and said prosaically, 'I hope I don't disturb you too much, getting up and down in the night.'

His fingers pressed into her hip then caressed her belly, silencing her with their touch as the air was sucked from her lungs and a wild longing to make love with him again suffused her body.

Breathe! Do the exercises.

She drew in air, forced it out, did it again, and again.

It was OK to be close to Angus, OK to enjoy his touch, she told herself as she kept up the rhythmic breathing.

But was it?

What of the future?

Could they work things out between them?

Get back together again for more than just a night?

Only if they could resolve 'the baby business'.

She half smiled into the darkness as she mentally used the phrase which had so infuriated her when Angus had said it. They'd both changed since then, hopefully matured.

Enough to sit down and talk about the future without the shadows of the past tainting what was said, without blame and recrimination souring the tattered remnants of their love?

The answers to this and all her questions were somewhere in her head but she was drifting off to sleep and couldn't sort the words into the right order, so she snuggled back against Angus and let the darkness come.

Angus felt her body relax and knew she was asleep. He needed sleep himself—tomorrow would be a working day. A day of discovery, too, he hoped.

He slid his palm flat against Jenessa's stomach and wondered if it mattered. If he really wanted to know. Felt a movement and began to imagine Jenessa's child instead—a tiny girl, dark-haired like her mother.

His heart jolted in reaction to the image. Of course he'd love Jenessa's baby. The knowledge was like a bright light shining in his mind, blotting out all fears and doubts.

But how could he convince Jen, when he'd been so adamant about not wanting a child only twelve months earlier?

He drifted off to sleep, half-formed sentences and protestations clamouring in his head.

She was gone when he awoke, and he vaguely remembered stirring when she'd moved away from him in the shadowy pre-dawn. He glanced at the clock and saw it was after seven. Heavens! If she was still following her old schedule—their old schedule—she'd be leaving the house at half past.

As he scooted into the bathroom she called to him from the kitchen, something about leaving later—he had an hour.

'I don't start before nine these days,' she explained when he joined her in the kitchen and helped himself to cereal. 'If I'm in by eight-thirty, it gives me time to read through test results and reports, before tackling patients for the day.'

She swung around from the sink, where she was rinsing her breakfast bowl, and hesitated, eyeing the crumpled shirt he'd grabbed from his bag and pulled on over his boxers.

'The clothes you left in the spare bedroom are hanging in the big closet. The shirts should be relatively clean as I washed them before I hung them up again. I had the place sprayed before I began my renovating and didn't know how much residue might have stuck to the fabric.'

It was a wifely thing for her to have said and he thanked her gravely although she'd already turned away as if the simple task of wiping a bowl took all her concentration. Wifely was good, but his heart wanted the lover back as well as the wife, and so far he'd seen precious little of the lover. Although she had asked him to share the bed…

And yesterday's kiss in the kitchen had been hotter than the fires of hell…

She half turned and he noticed the pinkness in her cheeks. Surely she couldn't have been thinking…

He reached out and took her hand.

'We have to talk, you know.'

Watched her nod agreement, her cheeks growing pinker by the second.

'I know,' she whispered, and he *knew* she was remembering the kiss, feeling the same flush of excitement he was feeling, their senses reclaiming each other, need spiralling out of control. All thought of talking vanished as he stood up and took her in his arms, fitting his body to hers before bending to claim her lips.

She met his demands with her own, her tongue tussling with his as if the taste of him was a requisite for life, more urgently needed than air or water. Tiny sounds issued from her throat, driving his own excitement towards frenzy. Her hands busied themselves against his body, plucking at the crumpled shirt, kneading into his muscles, lips now sucking at his skin.

His passion rose, the need so strong he could feel himself shaking with it, though uncertainty still dogged him and inner voices whispered that sex wasn't the answer, but a temporary release.

He renewed his assault on her lips, mentally arguing that anything they both wanted so much couldn't be all wrong, that this was one way they could come together— perhaps heal the wounds of the past and prepare the way for them to face the future.

Her response took what little breath he'd managed to drag into his heat-seared lungs, leaving him in little doubt as to how she felt.

'Are there rules about sex this late in pregnancy?' he whispered as she dragged his shirt open and flattened her hands against his skin.

'I can't remember!' she wailed, lips now close to his ear. 'I didn't take any notice of those bits of the book— didn't have to know.'

He could hear a potent mix of distress and desire in her voice, feel it in the trembling body pressed so close to his. He settled his hands on her shoulders and held her still as he raised his head and looked down into her eyes.

'Well, it's just as well we're out of time. We have to go to work, remember? Some time during the day one of us will look it up, OK?'

He watched the emotions shifting in her eyes—desire, then disbelief, regret, and, no, not shame!

'Hey, we shared a great love life, Jen,' he said gently. 'It's natural our bodies should react this way when they're reunited.'

'But I'm nearly nine months pregnant,' she muttered, so obviously angry with herself he had to kiss her once again, but as a friend this time, not a lover.

'Being pregnant doesn't completely obliterate a woman's hormonal urges,' he reminded her. 'That much learning I have retained.'

She broke away from him, picking up his cereal bowl and once again busying herself at the sink.

*   *   *

How could Angus have kissed her like that and half an hour later greeted his former colleagues as if nothing had happened, she wondered as she shut herself in her consulting room and tried to make sense of Mrs Franklin's latest blood test.

Why had she ordered blood urea when she was interested in her patient's oestrogen levels?

Jenessa stared at the piece of paper, but all she saw was Angus's face as he'd lifted his head and asked her about sex in pregnancy.

Concentrate!

She began to read again and saw it was Mr Lipski's blood test she was studying, not Mrs Franklin's. She pulled herself together as she realised the high level of urea could mean kidney disease—and definitely meant more tests were in order. But Mrs Franklin was her first patient. Where were her results?

Kathy came in as she was shuffling through the papers on her desk and dropped another pile of files on her desk.

'Typical Monday. Everyone putting up with their complaints over the weekend so they can mess up a weekday with a doctor's visit. How are things? Told him yet?'

She jerked her head towards the door to indicate who 'he' was.

Jenessa looked up and sighed. 'Not quite,' she said.

Kathy echoed the sigh then shook her head in disbelief. 'You two!' she muttered, then she walked back out of the room, leaving the door open so Jenessa could see Angus propped against the reception desk, chatting to Cindy, their practice nurse.

And beyond him, Mrs Franklin was coming through the outer door. No time to think about Angus now. She had to find the blood test.

'Ha!' She grabbed it from between the pages of Mr

Lipski's report and ran her fingers down the numbers she needed to read. It was easy to see as the pathology service had printed the abnormal serum oestrogen level in red. Now to persuade Mrs Franklin that taking supplemental oestrogen wasn't a crime against nature.

The door closed and she glanced up to see not her patient but Angus. Her heart greeted him with an acceleration which made her feel faint.

'Go away,' she said crossly, angry not at him but at her misbehaving heart.

'I thought this was a meet-the-patients session,' he said, smiling as if he knew exactly why she'd reacted as she had.

'Well, it is,' she stuttered, struggling to make up lost ground, 'but Mrs Franklin's come to see me because she wanted a woman doctor. She'll go back to Jack if she wants ''real'' medicine.'

Angus raised his eyebrows and smiled.

'Girl talk?'

'Something like that,' she mumbled, even more disconcerted now because her lungs had reacted to that smile.

'That's OK,' he said easily, and the smile became a mischievous grin, 'because there's something I want to look up. I was wondering how soon I'd get a few free minutes.'

Jen felt hot blood flowing up from her breasts, colouring her neck and staining her cheeks.

'Get out of here, Angus McLeod!'

She grabbed a book off the desk and lifted it as if to throw it, but he raised his hands in surrender—her medical self noticing the left one lifted higher than the right—and walked backwards out the door, pulling it shut behind him so she could no longer catch even a glimpse of him.

Which was fortunate, because just knowing he was in the same building was problem enough for her to handle. Not only in the building, but checking on what the experts had to say about—

Oh, hell!

She propped her elbows on the desk and dropped her head into her hands.

Honesty forced her to admit she wanted it as badly as he did, but weren't things complicated enough already?

A light tap on the door heralded Mrs Franklin, and with a major effort she shifted her attention from sex and Angus and, mentally composing herself, stood up to greet her patient.

Mrs Franklin enquired about Jen's health, talked about her own childbirth experience then finally allowed Jenessa to get down to business.

'Your oestrogen levels *are* low,' she told the older woman. 'Did you read the information about hormone replacement therapy I gave you?'

Mrs Franklin nodded then fished in her handbag and brought out the leaflet.

'What I don't understand is why my mother—all our mothers—didn't have this problem, all these problems.'

'They did,' Jenessa explained. 'Prior to the use of HRT women had the hot flushes and night sweats, all the problems you've described, but they simply accepted the discomfort as part of menopause. Now there's no reason for you to suffer if replacement therapy brings relief.'

'My mother didn't take it and she might have been uncomfortable but she didn't get osteoporosis, which this leaflet seems to think will happen to me if I don't go on the tablets.'

Jen shifted in her chair as a now-familiar contraction gripped her abdomen. She took a deep breath and released it slowly.

'Then you've chosen wisely with your parents,' she told Mrs Franklin, 'but osteo is still a risk. You have to remember that people, particularly women, are living longer now and as you grow older the risk of losing calcium from your bones increases. We see far more broken hips in eighty-year-olds than we do in sixty-year-olds.'

Mrs Franklin stared at her, eyes blank as she apparently digested this information.

'I see what you're getting at. My mother died in her sixties,' she announced. 'But what of side effects? What about breast cancer?'

It was the most repeated objection and Jenessa swallowed a sigh before she began her usual speech.

'There is no evidence to show there is an increased risk of breast cancer, although many people have done long-term studies on women taking hormone supplements. In fact, in one study done in the United States, the incidence in women on oestrogen alone was actually lower than would be expected in such a sample of the general population.'

'But you said I wouldn't take it on its own.'

Another pain, another swallowed sigh. Mrs Franklin had every right to ask these questions and was certainly doing the right thing, finding out all she needed to know before taking new chemicals into her body.

And she deserved a doctor who was equally interested in her concerns! Jenessa reminded herself.

'Since scientists decided to try hormone replacement in menopausal women, they've used various combinations. What they did find was that, by taking progesterone as well as oestrogen, the risk of breast cancer could decrease. It's also been shown that by adding progesterone, there are fewer side effects from the oestrogen, but it's not like putting you on one or two pills or even patches—there are a number of options you can choose, and we can adjust the levels of what we prescribe so it suits you as an individual.'

She smiled at her patient, sensing the woman's doubts remained.

'I know that all sounds terribly complicated, but it's really quite simple and the best thing to do is for you to try it for yourself. You don't have to commit to a lifetime of hormone replacement at this stage—just give it a go on a low dose and see if you feel any better. As well as the therapy, I'd recommend some regular exercise, even if it's only walking the dog.'

Mrs Franklin nodded, then she shook her head.

'When are you stopping work?' she asked, but Jenessa couldn't answer as another pain had grabbed her, more severe than the first two.

Damn Braxton-Hicks!

'At the end of this week,' she managed to force out. 'Dr McLeod is back and he'll be taking my patients.'

Mrs Franklin beamed at her.

'Perhaps you could write on my card what you think I should take, then if I decide to go ahead I can come back and see him and he'll know what to give me.'

So much for shunting Angus out of the room so Mrs Franklin could have privacy! Jen should have remembered how adored he'd been among the female patients.

Well, right now he could have them. What she wanted was to go home and lie in a very hot bath. Perhaps then the pains would stop.

She made notes on the card in front of her then stood up to show Mrs Franklin to the door. Angus was propped against the reception desk chatting to Kathy, and Jen's patient made a beeline towards him, greeting him with loud cries of delight. Jenessa motioned to Mr Lipski to come in, then another pain seized her and she clutched at the doorframe for support.

Angus couldn't have had his full attention on Mrs Franklin's welcome-home speech, for he was by her side in seconds, supporting her back into the consulting room and lowering her carefully into a chair.

'Braxton-Hicks nothing—you're in labour, you stupid woman!'

He sounded so angry she had to smile, although the pain made it a weak effort.

'I'll be OK in a few minutes,' she assured him, but she held onto his hand and leaned her head against his arm, pleased to have his support no matter how cross he was.

'Sit right there while I see Jack, then I'm taking you to hospital.'

His hand was cold and clammy, or was that hers? She tightened her fingers on it.

'We're at the hospital,' she reminded him. 'If it is the real thing all I have to do is walk across the road.'

'You won't walk anywhere,' he growled, the fingers of his free hand stroking her hair, lifting the strands and letting them fall. 'Just sit tight while I talk to Jack.'

She shouldn't let him organise her life like this, but right now, although she knew she wasn't ready to go across to the hospital, she did want to go home. She could have a bath then go to bed and stay curled up there until she was feeling better. Instinct told her this was a false alarm, but getting Angus to believe it might be difficult.

He unlatched his hand, gave her a final pat on the head and a firm admonishment to stay put, then he disap-

peared. She knew it was unfair on her partners to walk
out right now, and that, given time, she could probably
finish her day's work, but the emotional toll of Angus's
return was beginning to take effect and in between the
pains she felt weak and depressed. Definitely curling-up-
in-bed time!

'OK, it's all fixed. Kathy will phone the non-urgent
cases and I can see them later in the week. Those already
here, or who need to come in, will be split between
Neville and Jack.'

Angus put out his hand to help her to her feet. 'I've
even got a wheelchair to push you across to the hospital.'

She was on her feet by the time he made this an-
nouncement and she snatched her hand away.

'I'm not going to the hospital either on foot or in your
precious wheelchair,' she told him. 'I'll take the day off
because I'm not feeling well, but I'm going home to have
a hot bath and go back to bed.'

The pains had eased and she stepped away from him
because, pain-free, her body was finding other interests.

'And you can stay here and take my patients. Cindy
can find anything you need, and Jack and Neville will
act as back-ups.'

His lovely eyes scanned her face and she could see by
his stormy expression just what he thought of this sug-
gestion. In a way, she was touched by his concern, and
even more deeply affected by his panicky response. She
touched him on the arm.

'I will be OK!' she promised. 'I'll go home and rest,
and not do anything stupid.'

He opened his lips as if to put forward another argument, then shut them again, lifting his hand and once
again smoothing her hair.

'May I call you a cab?' he asked, a wry smile twisting

his well-shaped mouth. 'You shouldn't risk driving when
you're likely to have another cramp.'

She returned his smile.

'You can call me a cab,' she agreed, then she stretched
up and kissed him on the cheek. 'I'm glad you're here,'
she added softly, lifting her gaze to meet his and letting
the love she felt for him shine briefly in her eyes.

CHAPTER EIGHT

ANGUS managed to see a dozen patients before anxiety made him switch some to Jack so he could drive home to check on Jenessa. He hadn't wanted to phone in case she was sleeping, but concern had turned to a queasiness in his stomach and his mind had trouble concentrating on medical jargon and competent diagnoses.

He entered through the back door, and saw the red light blinking on the alarm. Remembering the drama of the previous evening, he slid his key into the slot to turn it off then walked quietly down the hall.

The silence suggested that Jenessa was asleep and he was obscurely pleased she'd taken the precaution to set the alarm although she'd been feeling so unwell.

Turning the knob as quietly as possible, he pushed open the bedroom door, but the bed, though still rumpled as evidence she'd slept in it recently, was empty.

Panic clutched at his intestines as he dashed towards the bathroom, certain he'd find her slumped unconscious on the floor—or, worse still, in the bath.

No one!

Panic gave way to anger. How dared she frighten him like this? And where could she have gone?

'The hospital? They were real contractions!'

He said the words aloud, trying to stop the new torment gnawing in his belly. Headed for the kitchen. He'd phone John Flynn, find out if she'd been admitted.

The note was on the kitchen bench, an A-4 sheet of

133

paper too large for him to miss if he'd bothered to glance that way earlier.

'Feeling better, walking on the beach.'

Well, she might feel better, but he certainly didn't. How could she cause him such anxiety?

Fury lent wings to his feet and he marched towards the sliding doors, flung them open and was halfway across the patio before he remembered the break-ins. He'd better lock the damn place.

It felt foolish to be taking these precautions when they were only likely to be away a few minutes, but he walked back inside, bolted the sliding doors, then checked his keys were in his pocket and went out through the back door, locking it behind him.

On the top of the dunes he hesitated. The soft, silvery sands of the beach stretched north and south. He strained his eyes and picked up a solitary figure, way to the north. It might or might not be her, but in the middle of a week-day the area was relatively deserted, other swimmers and sunbathers in small clumps.

With determined strides he headed north, his mind rehearsing all the things he wanted to say to her—like, how could she worry him this way and how stupid it was to walk alone and—

The practice dissipated his anger, or perhaps it was the wet, salt air he was breathing, and the soothing wash of the waves across the sand. Countless times he and Jen had wandered along this beach, sometimes hand in hand, at other times close but not touching, wrapped securely in the warm cocoon of their love. Here on the beach, from the earliest days of their courtship, they had shared their innermost secrets, their hopes, dreams and desires, or moved as one, their thoughts in silent communion with each other.

He tried to remember if she had talked of babies, but knew if she had he had probably let it drift pass his ears. He would have concentrated only on the things that were of more immediate interest, or, as with most humans, on those which were of importance to himself.

The solitary walker was drawing nearer and he realised he or she had turned around. Instinct told him it was Jenessa and he stepped up his pace, confirming his guess as he drew closer.

She must have recognised him at about the same time for she hurried forward, making him so fearful for her he forgot he'd been annoyed earlier. He waved his hands and called, 'There's nothing wrong. I was coming to meet you.'

'But the patients?' she objected, ever the professional.

He reached her side and took her arm to give her some support.

'I saw all your morning appointments and left Jack and Neville to handle any last-minute arrivals. Apparently, Kathy's been leaving you relatively free for a few hours at lunchtime, persuading all but the most insistent to see one of the other doctors.'

She looked startled, then shook her head. 'I should have guessed. They've all cosseted me something dreadful since I first told them. I was aware I was coming home less tired lately, but had been too involved in getting on with things to work out why.'

He slowed his pace, taking shorter steps to match hers, and relished the weight of her against him. He wanted to tell her again of his love, but knew the situation was too complicated for a 'love conquers all' scenario.

'What were your plans?' she asked, looking not at him but out across the rolling breakers towards the deep indigo of the ocean. 'Before you arrived and took on the dual role of nursemaid and locum.'

To woo and win you, was the simple answer. And now he'd been asked, he realised he hadn't thought much past that one objective.

'No plans,' he lied, for, although the wooing seemed unnecessary since he'd seen the love Jen still felt for him glowing in her eyes this morning, he was uncertain about the winning. About the prize.

'Well, I suppose you have to get your shoulder fixed, and regain your general health before you can think about the future.' The words were typical of his practical Jenessa, but he sensed a sadness in them. 'You don't *have* to take my place at work. The agency will find another locum.'

'I've made an appointment to see Allan about my shoulder. That's for early next week and, in the meantime, I'm happy to fill in for you,' he told her, although he'd realised soon after his arrival at the surgery his plan to learn the fatherhood of Jenessa's baby wasn't going to succeed. Without saying anything, the staff had given the impression they'd taken oaths of secrecy regarding that situation, and although he'd sensed a coolness among some of them he'd also felt there was more to it than anyone chose to reveal.

'Can we talk about us?' he asked.

'Is there an us?' she countered.

He stopped walking and turned so he could look into her eyes.

'Could there be, as far as you're concerned?'

She sighed, frowned, then lifted her hand and traced his lips with her forefinger, before moving it lower to run along his jaw.

'I love you, Angus,' she said, but her voice was full

of sorrow not joy. 'I suppose I always will. But if there's one thing I've learned from the past, it's that a marriage needs more than love if it's to survive. Not a lot, perhaps, but at least some common goals, a shared vision of its future and a commitment to that vision.'

Her words chilled him. The love he'd seen in her eyes—and now heard her admit—didn't mean the winning would follow. He bent and brushed his lips against hers then straightened up again and began to walk as if the movement would help him explain.

'Before I left Paris I told a friend about our marriage. About your "happy family" vision and my reaction to it. He asked why you hadn't shared it with me earlier in our marriage.'

He stopped again, and looked into her eyes.

'I did admit you probably had, and that I hadn't listened, but walking on the beach today, I could almost hear the words.' He paused, wondering whether a full confession would make things better or worse. 'I know how I'd have reacted—back then—because, subconsciously, I didn't want to get into the "happy families" thing. I pushed the idea away—ignored it—banished it from my mind.'

He saw hurt battle understanding in her face, then she said quietly, 'It's still my dream, my vision of the future, Angus.'

'And am I there—in this dream, this vision?'

She turned away, lifting her skirt and walking into a shallow wave, kicking her feet to make the water spray up like an arc of sun-sparkled diamonds.

'You always were, to use your words, "back then",' she said, looking not at him, but at the water swirling around her feet. 'Now it's up to you. You have to want it, perhaps not as fervently as I do, but enough to understand that it won't always be easy. That's where commitment comes in. And you have to believe, as I do, that love isn't a finite bundle which diminishes when it's spread around. I don't have to take back a bit of the love I give to you in order to have some for a child. As I see it, love expands exponentially, and the more we give the more it grows, so everyone within its magic circle will gain, not lose.'

She walked out of the water and he took her arm again.

'Your love works that way, Jen,' he admitted. 'I think the fairy godmother who attended your christening sprinkled you with enough love dust to encompass the entire world.'

'Perhaps,' she agreed, and he knew she'd say no more about the future, either hers, or his, or even theirs. It was now up to him to decide if he wanted in or out, if he wanted the 'two for the price of one' package she'd mentioned earlier.

Angus loved her and wanted her—that much was undeniable—and he sensed that the parentage of the child she carried no longer mattered. After the hamster test, they'd discussed artificial insemination using donor sperm, so a minor adjustment in his way of thinking and he could handle that part. What brought him up short was the image of the boy he'd been, separated from his sister and his mother, given to a father who'd taken him out of spite not love.

Jenessa asked about Mr Lipski, turning the talk back to safe medical topics which took them all the way home. Her steps slowed as they climbed the dune in front of the house, and he became aware that every step she took was an effort.

'You're still getting pains,' he scolded.

'No,' she argued, 'just finding it difficult to expand my lungs—there's too much else in the way.'

They reached the patio and stopped for her to catch her breathe.

'Sit here,' he said. 'I'll go around the back and open up.'

He steadied her as she subsided into a chair, then hurried around the house, concerned she might have overdone it, wondering how she'd know when the contractions finally meant the curtain was going up on the main event.

At first his brain didn't connect to what the open door meant, then, with an oath, he flew up the steps, bursting into the house, roaring threats at whatever intruders he might find inside. In one mad rush he hurtled down the hall, saw at a glance there was no one in the living room or kitchen and charged into the bedroom. It, too, had been vacated, although the evidence of a hasty search was everywhere, drawers pulled out of chests, clothes flung in disarray across the floor.

The mess made him pause and he bent down and picked up the red dress Jen had worn the previous day, holding it to his face, inhaling the lingering scent of her body. Then his fingers tightened on the material as images of someone breaking in while she was sleeping slapped into his mind.

Without pausing to think of danger to himself, he shot through the bathroom and back into the hall, glancing into the study then stopping dead as a muffled noise sounded from the spare bedroom.

Common sense returned. If the intruder was still lurking there, shouldn't he arm himself?

With what?

He tiptoed into the kitchen and picked up the broom—

a feeble weapon but better than nothing. Treading quietly, he inched along the wall of the hall, then he raised his foot and kicked at the door to fling it open.

No flinging, just a general sag to one side. The door had already been kicked, the lock broken in the assault.

And the noise came from Jenessa, soft whimpers of distress as she stood, tears streaming down her cheeks, and surveyed the havoc the intruder had wrought in the room she'd so lovingly prepared for her baby.

Hot waves of rage broke through Angus's body, compounded by a need to stop Jenessa's pain. He reached out and put his good arm around her shoulders.

'Come on, darling,' he murmured, turning her so he could steer her out of the room. 'Don't look at it, don't upset yourself with it. Let's get out of here.'

He edged her out then remembered how the bedroom looked and knew she couldn't take another shock so he walked her through to the lounge and sat her down, easing her onto the couch so her head was propped on one end and her feet on the other. She let him arrange her, as limp as a rag doll, her body shuddering from time to time but not resisting his attention.

He put the kettle on, then phoned the police, made tea for Jenessa and waited while she drank some of it.

'I think your exercise partner would recommend deep breathing,' he suggested, knowing if she slept she could forget the horror for a while.

She smiled wanly up at him, but obediently breathed in, sighing out the air then repeating the exercise. Her eyelids drooped and he wondered if some autonomic response was shutting down her thoughts, protecting her from more pain.

When he was sure she was OK, he left, heading first

for the bedroom. Did the police have to see this disarray?
Would they take fingerprints?

Did it matter?

Well, that was one question he could answer. He
would be careful not to touch anything but the clothes,
but when Jen was ready to move it was to this room she'd
be coming and he wasn't going to let her walk into this
mess.

He grabbed his camera first and took a photo in case
how it looked was important, then he picked up, folded
or hung, restoring the room to order. The bathroom was
easier. Everything had been pulled out of the small cabinet, bottles and jars smashed on the floor, but he didn't
feel the sense of personal invasion he'd experienced in
the bedroom so he left it as it was for the moment.

In the study, the contents of the desk drawers were
tipped in haphazard piles on the floor but, again, it didn't
make him want to belt someone as the bedroom scene
had. He turned away, walking towards the last room in
the house, hoping it wasn't as bad as his first mental
images of it had made it seem.

It wasn't as bad, it was worse. Looking at the torn
drapes, the scattered and disfigured toys, the overturned
crib and slashed mattress, Angus felt the rage of madness.
Not his own this time, but that of the person who'd
wreaked such devastation.

He felt fear, then gratitude that Jenessa had not been
here, and while he was trying to isolate the other emotions churning in his chest, the image of Jenessa's infant,
the tiny, black-haired girl he'd pictured in his mind,
sprang into his head. How could anyone do this to that
baby—Jen's baby—*his* baby?

The thought liberated his own anger, but it was cold,
not hot, this time, and it cleared the fog of confusion

through which he'd struggled, allowing him to catch a glimpse of Jenessa's vision of the future.

The policeman who came greeted him familiarly, looked at the destruction and shook his head.

'What's been taken?' he asked. 'Anything obvious like video recorder or TV?'

'I know it sounds stupid, but I haven't looked. In fact, I wouldn't know, apart from the obvious.' They were standing in the hall so he turned and saw the television set and video in their proper places in the living room. Saw Jenessa still asleep—or pretending to be so she didn't have to face reality just yet. 'Nothing seems to be missing,' he said, 'but I'll check later and give you a list.'

'Your wife's a doctor. Any drugs on the premises?'

It was Angus's turn for head-shaking.

'We had a special compartment built into the boot of the car, where the spare fits, and keep our medical bag in there. It's not visible if anyone pops the lid open, and means we don't have to stow it anywhere in the house.'

'That's what they were looking for,' the policeman guessed. 'You only have to glance around that big room to see there's no bag there, so they hauled stuff out of bedroom cupboards, searching for it, went through the bathroom cabinets for any small drug samples you might have stashed away, checked the study drawers for cash, then found the locked door. There's nothing as suspicious, or enticing, to your friendly neighbourhood burglar as a locked door.'

'So they kicked it in! It seems impossible. This is an old house, but it's been solidly built.'

'Check the hinges. They're probably ripped out of the doorframe.'

Angus sighed.

'OK, I can go with kicking in the locked door, but why, when they found it was a baby's room, would they do that to it?'

The policeman glanced that way and frowned.

'Frustration? Anger? They'd expended a lot of energy, getting it open, then to find it full of frills and baby stuff, full of love, I suppose, which they might not have had as kids…'

He let the words trail away, but understanding the mis-creants' motives failed to soothe Angus's anger at who-ever had done this to Jenessa.

'You're talking about "they" as if you can tell there was more than one,' he said, following the policeman out through the back door and around to the side of the house.

'Well, two's an educated guess. You're not high off the ground, but once they had a window open it'd be easier to get in if one gave the other a boost up, then he or she opens a door. Usually two doors, front and back, so they've got a quick exit it anyone returns.'

Angus thought back to his return, to the silence in the house, hurrying to the front doors. Had they been un-locked?

He couldn't recall then realised that if they had been, he'd have assumed Jen had left them that way.

When she'd set the alarm?

The question clanged in his head with the resonance of a strong drumbeat.

Alarm.

The anger he'd felt for the unknown intruder now turned inward, and his gaze followed the policeman's pointing finger to the study window where a broken panel revealed how the intruders had managed to get in.

'I walked down to the beach and didn't reset the alarm,' he muttered.

'Look, mate,' the policeman said, walking on to complete his circumnavigation of the house, 'unless the neighbours were at home on either side, no one would have heard it or, if they had, taken much notice. Alarms are to frighten the thieves away. When they hear the noise, instinct tells them to run, but most professionals, and even semi-professionals, know the noise stops in minutes and it always takes longer than that for the police or security people to arrive, given the alarm is connected to the station or a security firm, which very few are.'

The prosaic words did little to lighten Angus's burden of guilt as he continued to follow the policeman's route.

'I'll send someone to dust the window and the bathroom cabinet. If they've left prints, we'll find them there. I doubt your wife wants fingerprint powder through the rest of the house.' He closed his notebook and turned to offer Angus his hand. 'If it's any consolation, having come once and not found drugs, these particular culprits are unlikely to return.'

'Oh, great, I can expect new villains next time,' Angus said gloomily.

'I doubt it.' The policeman paused on his way out to the lane and waved his hand towards the vacant lot behind the house. 'We've been notified that construction on that site starts next week. Big apartment block going up. There's nothing like a building site to keep the miscreants away from neighbouring property. Building workers learn to watch what's going on around them and they'll have a bird's eye view of your place.'

Well, that's some comfort, Angus decided as the official drove away. At least I won't be quite so paranoid when Jen is at home with a newborn baby.

But the guilt he felt still dominated and he was wondering where to begin the reclamation of the house when a loud yell made him glance up the lane. Stick was approaching on a bicycle, one arm waving in case his cry hadn't caught Angus's attention.

'That police car was here, wasn't it? Is Jenessa OK?'

Trust the youth to think of her first.

'She's upset,' Angus said bluntly. 'Another break-in and they trashed the baby's room.' He spoke gloomily then realised that Stick could be his saviour. 'Look, she's inside, lying down, but I want to clean up as much mess as I can without her having to look at it again. Can you take her into your place and look after her? Don't leave her alone because she's shocked and upset and wasn't feeling too well before all this happened.'

'I'll watch her,' Stick promised, his usual belligerence missing, his voice husky with concern for his friend.

Angus nodded, his suspicion of the young man—his jealousy of his place in Jen's life—totally erased by that simple promise.

'The baby's room is the worst,' he told Stick as he led the way back into the house. He would have liked to warn him but couldn't find words to describe the horror of it.

'Bastards!'

The lad's oath, repeated again and again, said it all. He stood transfixed, shaking his head, as if the image his eyes presented to him was too horrifying to be believed.

Angus took his arm and drew him forward.

'I'll put it right,' he promised. 'Perhaps later, if Carole is at home, you could come back and tell me where Jen bought some of the things.'

'I know the paint colour,' Stick offered. 'And there's some left for touching up in the shed.'

Jen was sitting on the lounge, looking pale and bewildered. She turned as they entered.

'Oh, Jason, did you see what they did?' The words were a cry of despair.

Angus reached her first and sat down beside her, wrapping her in his arms.

'We'll fix it,' he promised. 'I'll put it right, Jen. Now, Stick's going to take you over to his place while I clean up here.'

He expected her to protest and when she didn't he realised how emotionally exhausted she must be. First his return, now this—and at the end of her pregnancy when the foetus was making more and more demands on her system.

He helped her up and watched Jason put his arm around her shoulders. Caught the sheen of tears in the young man's eyes, and turned tactfully away to open the front door for them. From what he'd gathered, Stick had put as much of his time, effort and love into that room as Jenessa had. He, too, needed time to mourn its destruction.

As they walked away, he glanced at his watch and realised he should be back at work. He lifted the phone and rang the surgery, where Jack assured him they could cope and told him to phone Nellie, who'd been the chief decorating consultant on the baby's room.

By the time Nellie arrived, the fingerprint man had been and Angus had restored order to the study—although the papers would have to be sorted out later—and had the bedroom almost back to rights. He was ordering new glass for the study window when she called a greeting.

A hug of welcome, shattered cries of denial when she saw the wreckage, then she was all business.

'I'll take the curtains and bedclothes with me, match the material on the way home and get my mum to sew the new ones. How soon do you want them?'

Angus hesitated, looking slowly around the room. He remembered Jen's distress and knew it wouldn't be eased by a half-finished job.

'By tomorrow morning?' he begged. 'I know it's a lot to ask, but she was so distraught, so shocked, I have to get it right by morning. At the moment, she's too wiped out to argue about staying next door overnight, but you know Jenessa. She'll start fretting to come home the moment the emotional upheaval begins to settle, and I don't want her to see it even in a half-finished state.'

He could hardly bear to look at it himself, or think of the dark-haired baby in the devastation of this room.

Nellie stared at him.

'You care!' she said in such accusing tones he was shocked out of his maudlin mood.

'Of course I care. I've always cared about Jen.'

'It's more than that,' Nellie told him. 'You, of anyone, know how tough Jenessa is. You're upset because they wrecked the baby's room!'

Angus shrugged, uncomfortable now his thoughts had been spoken.

'Anyone would be,' he muttered, and Nellie smiled.

'Well, if you need a miracle, find me a couple of plastic bags. You take the curtains down and I'll gather up the toys. I should be able to replace most of them, and what I can't I'll substitute. And while I'm at the store, I'll order new mattresses for the bassinet and crib, and have them delivered this afternoon. You can't put new carpet down at this stage because the fumes from it could affect the baby, but I'll see if they've got a mat that would fit in with the colour scheme. You can put it over the stain.'

She pointed to where something, possibly sterilising liquid, had been tipped on the floor.

'Thanks, Nellie,' Angus said, and gave his friend a hug. 'I probably wouldn't have noticed it until it was too late to do anything about it.' He hesitated, thinking of the newborn babies he'd seen in hospitals, swaddled in wrappings.

'Do you think you could get new sheets and shawls and all that kind of thing? I think, if I were Jen, I wouldn't want the baby wrapped in anything those people have touched. I'll fix you up for whatever you spend. Insurance will cover most of it.'

Nellie looked at him for a minute, then nodded as if satisfied with what she'd seen.

'You'll do,' she said briskly, then she waved him away, demanding plastic bags.

He found a few and returned to the room to find her writing a list. She showed it to him then handed him a card with a mobile number printed on it. While he took down the curtains, she read the list to him. It seemed a mile long.

'I haven't included baby clothes, although what Jen had already bought seems to be strewn around the place. I warned her not to buy much as people always give baby clothes as presents and you end up with too many. If you perform your miracle by morning, you'll deserve a day off work. Once you've caught up on your sleep, you and Jen could go shopping and replace the clothes together.'

Her words hit him like a fist in the solar plexus. It was one thing to picture Jen with a baby in her arms, to imagine the little scrap of humanity, but shopping for clothes for it?

'There's nothing decided,' he said stiffly.

'Oh, no?' Nellie teased. 'All Jen's looking for is commitment to the idea of "family", and fixing this room by morning fair reeks of that sweet virtue. Phone me if you think of anything else you need,' she continued, then she kissed him on the cheek, and added, 'I've always thought, for all your protests to the contrary, you had the makings of a good father.'

She walked away while he was still absorbing the impact of her words, then he realised it was time for action, not thought. Get everything out of the room, clean down the walls, paint them first and then, while they dry, fix the damaged door and furniture. He'd ask Stick about—

Commitment to the idea of 'family', Nellie had said. He inserted himself into the image of Jen and the infant, and shook his head. Then smiled.

CHAPTER NINE

'YOU there, Angus?'

He heard the voice and footsteps at the same time. Stick was returning, and from the savoury smell preceding him, he'd brought dinner.

'Pizza delivery and the mail,' the lad announced, going on to the kitchen as Angus emerged from the bedroom. 'Carole's sorting through her wardrobe, which didn't interest Jenessa much at first until she realised how huge Carole's wardrobe is and how much gear she was chucking out. Now they're magging about which of the rejects might suit Jenessa when she's back to normal size.'

As Angus watched, Stick slapped slices of pizza onto two plates, then thrust the rest of it, box and all, into the oven.

'Might need more nosh later,' he explained. 'How're you doing?'

Angus pushed the pile of mail along the bench, and sat down to tackle the food.

'Not as well as I'd hoped, although I've cleaned up the bathroom and I've washed most of the graffiti off the walls. I couldn't lift the cot out by myself, so I've worked around that.'

He saw the shudder that ripped through Stick's body and knew he was remembering how the room had looked.

'What was that stuff on the walls? Was it—?'

'Thankfully, no!' Angus cut in. 'I thought that's what it was, but there was no smell. They'd been in the bathroom first and smashed all the jars in the cabinet. Jen had

150

some body scrub, and they'd scooped out handfuls of it and smeared that across the walls, as well as the contents of tubes of nappy-rash cream and whatever else they could find in the baby's room. The red was lipstick from the bathroom. I've worked out most of what they used from the empty containers littering the floor.'

'What next?' Stick asked.

'Painting, so it has time to dry. I found the touch-up paint and had the hardware store deliver more in the same colour, as well as a new tin of white enamel. I thought I'd cover the marks I can't get out first, then, when that dries, repaint the walls.'

'You can't do that with your busted shoulder,' Stick argued.

'You watch me!' Angus replied. 'I can use a roller with my left hand and I've got an assistant for the brush stuff.'

Stick grinned at him.

'Let's get started, then.'

Four hours later they warmed up the remaining pizza slices and snacked on them while they planned the next move.

'I had a look at the little basket thing the baby will use when it first comes home, and it's not damaged at all,' Stick offered. 'But the bastards have kicked the cot and busted bits of the frame. I don't know how you're going to fix that, and as for the rocking chair…'

Angus recalled Jen saying Stick had bought her the chair and understood the gloom in the youngster's voice.

'Haven't you ever explored the shed?' he asked. 'Seen old Sid's workbench?'

Stick stood up, staring at Angus as if the work had affected his brain.

'There's a workbench out there, all right, but having a workbench and fixing things, that's different.'

Angus finished his pizza, washed it down with the last mouthful of a glass of milk and said, 'Follow me and all will be revealed.'

He led the way out to the shed where the rocking chair and cot had been deposited earlier.

'See, up there in the rafters, there are odds and ends of timber in every conceivable shape and size. I bet we can find what we need for our repairs and if we can't, then look here.' He unlocked and flung open the doors of a tall metal cabinet in which were hung power-tools of every description.

'When old Sid sold the place to us, he was going into a retirement village and had no room for all his stuff, not that he'd used it for years as his eyesight was going. Anyway, for an extra thousand dollars, I got the lot. Jen thought I was mad, but I knew the old bloke was upset at having to sell his tools and I thought one day I might get interested in fixing things myself.'

'So, you've got all this gear and no idea how to use it!' Stick muttered, his disgust echoing in his voice.

'I've some idea,' Angus argued. 'About the only advantage of growing up with my father was that he had and used all these tools and, although I was never allowed to touch anything, I did get to watch.'

They set to work, deciding what they'd need to replace broken struts and supports. Angus directed the procedure while Stick poked through the timber stored across the beams of the big shed's roof.

Angus found himself enjoying Stick's company. The young man had opinions about most things and a ruthless honesty in expressing them. The only wariness between them was when Jenessa or the baby was mentioned, when the conversation would be steered sideways to something else.

By two in the morning they had repaired both the cot and the rocking chair and put a new coat of pristine white gloss paint on both of them. They had also repainted the small chest of drawers, which had suffered the same fate as the walls.

'Why don't you buzz off home and get some sleep?' Angus suggested, but Stick wasn't leaving.

'You'll never get these things back inside without me, man,' he pointed out. 'And, as well as that, I just remembered the frieze.'

Angus recalled hearing the word before but his mind was too tired and confused to work out when or in what connection.

'The freeze, as in cold?'

Stick laughed,

'No, different spelling. It's a little bitty roll of wallpaper you put around the room. Jenessa and I were going to do it at the weekend, but—'

Angus knew the obstacle had been his return, but the idea of the frieze intrigued him.

'I didn't come across it when I was throwing things out. Do you know where Jenessa would have put it?'

'Out here somewhere, I'd say. She kept all the paint and tools out here.'

Stick began to search along the shelves lining one wall of the shed, shrieking with delight when he found what he was seeking.

'Let's put it up. Does it come with foolproof directions?'

They went back into the house, and through to the kitchen for the bowl of warm water Stick said they would need. As the lad made the preparations, Angus leafed through the pile of mail, aware that most, if not all, of it would be for Jenessa. But there was one letter for him.

It was in an airmail envelope, the African address almost obliterated by postmarks and redirection orders.

The writing was Jenessa's. It was the letter she'd written him.

While Stick headed for the baby's room, Angus slit the envelope open and pulled out the two sheets of fine airmail paper. Jen's writing was small, the words squashed together, as if she'd had to compress a lot of information into a small space.

He hesitated, hefting the paper in his hands, wondering if now was the time to read what she'd written to him, deciding there were a lot of things he didn't want to learn. In his mind, the baby was now his. The act of restoring the room had secured its place in his heart and he didn't want to know any more than that. He heard Stick's voice but didn't, couldn't, answer as a multitude of emotions washed through him.

'I said I've got it all ready to go but I'll need a hand,' Stick announced, coming into the kitchen to hurry Angus along.

He looked from the letter to Angus's face, then reached out and picked up the envelope.

'You got it, then,' he said.

'I haven't read it,' Angus admitted, then he frowned at the lad. 'Somehow it doesn't matter any more.'

'You sure you don't want to read it?' Stick asked. As Angus shook his head, the teenager held out his hand and took the sheets of paper, tucking them into his shirt pocket.

'I'll keep it in case you change your mind,' he offered. 'She didn't want to write to you but those friends of hers and yours at work told her she had to let you know.' He shuffled his feet and hid a yawn. 'We should get this frieze thing up while it's wet. Can we talk later?'

With a kind of wonder, Angus realised his companion was offering to be there for him, as he'd been there for Jen while he, Angus, had been off pursuing his own dream. Rare empathy for a seventeen-year-old.

'OK, let's do the frieze,' he said. Getting to know Stick better, well, that could wait.

He followed the lad into the bedroom and saw the marks where his helper had measured up from the floor to give them a guide for the paper, and blurted out his request.

'Let's not tell Jen the letter's come back.' He held the end of paper Stick handed him and tried to explain. 'If she didn't want to write it in the first place, then why worry her by bringing up its return? For the present, could we leave things the way they are?'

Stick placed one end of the frieze against the wall and pressed it into position.

'As long as the two of you don't make a muck of things again, I'll stay out of it,' he said sternly. 'But you've got to get your act together, man, show the woman you care about the things she cares about. Hell, my family wasn't that crash hot but it stuck together. When my mum and dad were killed five years ago, aunts descended from everywhere and took care of me and Carole.

'OK, so I resented it and rebelled and did some dreadful things, but family's all you've got when bad stuff happens, and my family stuck by me, fighting off the officials who said I should be put in care and managing to keep me out of detention centres until I got my act together and realised I needed an education to get anywhere in life.'

It was the longest speech Angus had ever heard from

Stick, and threw a lot of light on the previously taciturn youngster's background.

They worked slowly around the room, putting the dainty depiction of frolicking bears into position.

'If we had the toys and things we could make it almost like it was,' Stick said when they were standing back to admire their handiwork.

'Have a look in the bedroom then give me a hand to get the furniture back in,' Angus told him. 'I might have to send you home as soon as it's light to keep Jen over there until the curtains and pretty bed things arrive, but we'll have it right—better even—by the time she sees it.'

Stick gave him a startled look then disappeared through the bathroom into the main bedroom, returning to give Angus a high five, and a delighted 'Yes, man!'

'I did have help,' Angus admitted, explaining that he wouldn't have worked out how to replace all the damaged items if Nellie hadn't appeared and organised things.

The thought of finishing lifted a little of the tiredness now dogging Angus's steps and eased some of the pain in his protesting shoulder. Together they set the furniture back in place, and Stick took on the task of arranging the toys and hanging the new mobiles from the ceiling.

'When you decided to do this,' he said to Angus as they surveyed the all but finished room, 'was it for Jenessa or for the baby?'

Angus looked at him.

'For Jenessa first because she was so shattered by what had happened it seemed the only way I could make her whole again, but I was angry for the baby's sake. That someone could do this to her room.'

'You think it's a her?' Stick asked. 'I kinda hoped it might be a boy. I was going to teach him to surf.'

'You can teach a girl to surf,' Angus said softly, and he put his good arm around his new friend's shoulders and led him out through the living room to the front door where the light in the eastern sky proclaimed the arrival of the new day.

'We need a signal,' he said. 'What if I hang a towel out the bedroom window when it's all finished? Do you think you can stay awake long enough to keep Jenessa at your place until that's done?'

'I'll make her do her exercises if she argues,' Stick promised. 'That usually sends her off to sleep for a short time, no matter how early it is.' He turned towards Angus as if there was more he wanted to say, then he shrugged awkwardly and said, 'I'd better have a shower and get into pyjamas before she wakes. If she sees these clothes and smells the paint, it'd be a dead give-away.'

He crossed the space between the houses with long strides, seemingly inexhaustible, while Angus wondered how he'd manage to stay awake until Nellie arrived.

Not that he had to. He, too, could shower and change, then doze until she arrived.

An hour later, loud knocking roused Angus from a deep sleep. So much for dozing, he muttered to himself as he made his way to the door to let in not only Nellie but her mother.

'Well, young man, I hope you've got your part of the job done. I was up till midnight, fixing these,' the older woman said.

He didn't answer, merely leading the two women down the hall and throwing open the door of the bed-room. It smelt of paint, but apart from that, looked as fresh and vibrant and welcoming as it had before the disaster.

'I can't believe it's the same room,' Nellie said, turning to him and giving him a hug. 'How on earth—?'

'I had help,' Angus admitted. 'In fact, there's no way I could have managed on my own.' As Nellie took over the curtain-hanging while her mother made up the cot and bassinet with new sheets and coverlets, he explained about Stick's contribution.

'Well, it's grand,' Nellie said, as they all admired the completed effort. 'And I'm glad you had help. Jack wanted to come down but I told him he'd be more use having a good night's sleep so he could cope with extra patients today.'

Angus nodded. 'It was a personal thing as well,' he admitted. 'Stick's been here for Jenessa, helped her create the room, so I couldn't not let him help. But it was something that had to be my effort as well, my gift to Jen, in a way.'

'And you'll be wanting to show it to her no doubt,' Nellie said, and began to hustle her mother towards the door. 'We're out of here. Catch up with you soon.'

As soon as he heard the car engine start up, Angus grabbed a towel from the bathroom and hung it out the bedroom window. Excitement and anxiety churned inside him. He wanted to see Jenessa's reaction, to know she was OK.

Voices warned him of Jen's return and his body reacted to the idea with more inner unease.

He heard Stick tell her everything would be OK, that they'd fix the room, then she was there in the hall, and Angus pushed open the door.

The image of how the room had looked was so vivid in Jenessa's mind she all but yelled at Angus, then she saw how tired and strained he looked and muted the words.

'No, close it again, Angus. I can't bear to see it again.'

'You'd better look,' he growled. 'Stick and I didn't go without sleep to have you walk right past.'

She turned to Stick who blushed a bright scarlet and shuffled his feet, but said nothing. She glanced back at Angus, who was smiling now, although there was reserve behind that smile.

They'd have cleaned up the mess and tried to make good the damage. How could she tell them she didn't want her baby in a broken cot no matter how tidy they'd made the room?

'Have a look, Jen,' Angus challenged.

She took a deep breath, wrapped her hands protectively around her belly and stepped forward, peering reluctantly through the half-open door.

She saw the frieze first and turned to Stick, who motioned for her to go in. She stepped inside and looked around, shaking her head in disbelief. It was if the destruction of the previous day had never happened, a nightmare banished by morning light and the sight of this beautiful restoration. Walking further in, she touched the curtains, remembering the rips and tears she'd seen the day before.

'It's exactly as it was—better even, if you count the frieze. How did you do it?' she asked, turning to the two males who were standing in the doorway with silly smiles of pride and expectation on their faces.

'We had some help,' Angus admitted. 'Nellie shopped for all the replacements and her mother did the sewing. We didn't want the baby to have stuff the intruders had touched so Nellie bought new everything.'

'We didn't?' Jen repeated, looking hard at Angus, realising how much his answer meant to her.

'Well, I didn't,' he admitted. 'I told Nellie to give anything that wasn't damaged to a charity but I thought—'

She stepped forward and took his hand, grasped one of Jason's as well, and tried to thank them both. Later, when she was over this new emotional hurdle, she'd think through what Angus had said. She knew he still cared about her, but surely what must have been a Herculean task meant he cared about the baby. Would he be willing to take on her 'two for the price of one' package?

'I'm off to bed,' Jason announced. He withdrew his hand from Jen's then nodded towards Angus. 'And you should tuck him in for a few hours. He hasn't said anything but that shoulder must be giving him hell.'

Jen thanked him again and said goodbye, then turned to Angus, guilt overlying her delight in the room.

'He's right, you should be in bed. And you shouldn't have done it,' she scolded.

Now she looked properly at him, his face was grey with fatigue or pain, or possibly both.

'But you're glad we did?' he asked softly.

Once again, her voice choked on the words she wanted to say, so she kissed him on the cheek and mumbled a heartfelt, 'Yes!'

He put his arms around her and drew her close, nuzzling his face into her hair, then placing one hand on her belly and moving it as if to comfort the baby as well.

And, holding her like that, he spoke again.

'Nellie didn't replace any baby clothes,' he said, his voice sounding tight and unnatural—but that could be exhaustion, she decided. 'She thought you might prefer to do that yourself.'

He paused but she knew he hadn't finished, so she stood still within the circle of his arm, his hand smoothing her clothes where they bulged over her unwieldy bulk.

'Perhaps I could come with you,' he said, with more diffidence than she'd ever heard from Angus in all the years she'd known him.

She didn't know what to say, unable to believe this might mean their future lay together, although all the signs were pointing that way. But he'd gone onto the IVF programme to please her, his willingness propped up by a degree of guilt. Was this a similar reaction? Self-preservation warned her it could be, but her heart wanted to believe it was the first step towards the commitment she wanted from him.

No, the second step. The room had been the first—and a giant step at that.

'I'd love you to come,' she said softly, pressing a kiss against his neck and nibbling at his ear. 'But right now you need some sleep and I should go to work. Jack and Neville held the fort yesterday afternoon when I fell apart over all of this—I can't ask them to do the same again.'

'They won't mind,' he argued. 'You had a shock yesterday, you should rest.'

She smiled at his concern.

'I'm OK,' she assured him. 'One of the few advantages of being this pregnant is that the mind seems to go into a semi-comatose state. I can function normally at work and do routine things without any bother, but it shuts down on anything likely to throw me into a dither. Admittedly, it didn't work quite as quickly as it could have yesterday afternoon, but last night I slept OK. It's as if some drug my body is producing smooths out all the highs and lows and only leaves me with a kind of flat emotional plain.'

She moved out of the shelter of his arms.

'I'll have a quick shower and change into working gear, then the bedroom's all yours. Phone me when you wake up and we'll work out when I can get away to do some shopping.'

The thought quickened into excitement—perhaps the highs weren't completely levelled out—and she let it show, smiling at him, aware her eyes were glowing with the promise of the proposed expedition—and the togetherness of it.

He smiled back and dropped a kiss on her lips.

'I love you, Jen,' he said, but again she sensed the strain in his voice and wondered if she was rushing him, if the break-in had precipitated him into making a decision he hadn't completely considered.

At work, she accepted commiserations over the break-in, and advice that it was time she told Angus it was his child she was carrying. The urge to do so was strong, but she shelved her friends' arguments, still hesitant herself, too uncertain how he might react. What if it made him feel an obligation she didn't want to force on him?

The first appointment was with Mrs Gibson and she greeted the woman warmly, then flushed with pleasure as her patient handed her a small gift.

'For the baby!' Mrs Gibson explained. Jen unwrapped it then exclaimed over the exquisite embroidery on a tiny white nightgown.

Once thanks had been said, she consulted her patient's file and talked to her about the result of the sleep tests and possible treatment.

'There's a new laser technique to remove a small amount of flesh from the back of the throat,' Jen told her, pulling an illustration on the inside of a human mouth out of a drawer so she could show as well as tell. 'They've operated in the past, but the pain and recovery time following the operation made it a last-resort solution. Now, with a laser, you can have it done in day surgery and, apart from a feeling of being swollen there for a few days, will have few after-effects.'

'Is it expensive?' Mrs Gibson asked, and Jenessa sighed. It was a bugbear with her that people who could afford to pay more should get more efficient treatment.

'The specialist who's perfected the technique does a session a week at the public hospital. If you're interested, I can contact him and ask if he's doing it there and book you in if he agrees.'

'I'll agree,' Mrs Gibson said, so quickly she couldn't have given it more than a few seconds' consideration. 'My husband Dave is that fed up with all the snoring, he's shifted into the spare bedroom.' She looked down at her clasped hands for a moment, then looked up at Jen again, blushing slightly as she said, 'I'd like him back in bed with me again.'

It made Jen think of Angus and the despair she'd felt when he'd started sleeping in the spare bedroom. Yes, she wanted him back in her bed again as well. Badly enough to do just about anything to achieve it.

But now she had the baby to consider as well, she reminded herself as she made a note on Mrs Gibson's file. And its future, its mental health and long-term happiness.

'I'll get in touch when I've spoken to the surgeon,' she promised as she showed her patient out. 'And if I'm not here, one of the other doctors will contact you.'

She said goodbye, thanking Mrs Gibson again for the gift and her good wishes, then she glanced at the file she'd picked up off her desk, read the name and called her next patient in. She'd think about the future later. For now it was enough to know that Angus was going shopping with her.

CHAPTER TEN

BUT not that day. A series of crises kept Jenessa busy all morning and in the end she phoned Angus to apologise.

'Jack's got onto a doctor who's recently retired and he'll come in tomorrow morning. We'll go then.'

She wondered if it was wise, this expedition together when so much remained unresolved, but she could hardly back out now.

'OK. Now I'm up and about, I'll come into work and do what we'd intended doing yesterday—meet your patients.'

She didn't argue, feeling tired and out of sorts again, aware the upset of the previous day was now taking its toll.

They worked through till six, stopping on the way home at the Thai restaurant they'd frequented often in the past. Jenessa was content to let Angus fuss over her, ordering her off to the shower, heating milk for her to drink before she went to sleep.

In the big bed.

Knowing he'd be sleeping with her.

But even so, she slept uneasily, waking often, pain niggling at her body, so in the end she turned off the alarm and shifted to the spare bed so at least Angus could get a good night's sleep.

She was standing in the kitchen, wondering about food, when he awoke.

'What about a cup of tea and a slice of toast to keep

us going, then a real breakfast at a coffee-shop in the shopping centre before we shop?'

'A real breakfast? Like pancakes and maple syrup?' She grinned at him. Their favourite treat to each other had been going out to breakfast.

'And bacon,' he promised. 'Let's indulge ourselves for once. Overload the cholesterol for a change.'

His words were casual but Jen could feel a tension in the air, as if he was hiding something behind the light banter. And, although she'd felt his hand resting on her hip during the night, he'd made no move to kiss her again.

'Well, let's get this show on the road,' he added. 'I'll do tea and toast while you get showered and dressed, then I'll use the bathroom while you eat.'

Once we'd have showered together, she thought, then smiled as she realised how difficult that might be right now.

Half an hour later they were on their way.

'I set the alarm,' Angus assured her as he opened the car door for her.

'I do it out of habit,' she responded, realising he felt guilty about not having done it the day of the break-in, 'but when I had them installed, the consultant told me I should put security screens on the windows as well, because professionals know they have time after the alarm starts ringing and often wear earplugs to deaden the noise.'

Angus settled into the driver's seat and she sniffed the air, relishing the familiar clean-scented aftershave and the subtle maleness not totally obliterated by the chemical concoction. In so many ways, it was unbelievably wonderful to have him back again.

'Why didn't you get security screens?' he asked, and

she grinned to herself. Here she was, thinking of his body scent, while his mind was on security.

'Because they're awkward to fit on older houses with push-out windows and also…' She paused, uncertain if he'd understand. But Angus always had understood her—about most things. 'I didn't want to feel I *had* to.'

He grinned and patted her shoulder.

'Same old Jen, not liking to be manipulated by forces beyond your control. I felt that trait had a lot to do with your determination to get pregnant. How dare fate play you such a card? It made you determined to beat it. Yet, if you think about it, IVF must be the ultimate in manipulation, physically at least.'

She glanced at him to try to read his mood. There'd been no rancour in his voice, and she saw none in his face. It was a discussion, nothing more, without the heat and anger of others they'd had on the same subject.

Yet it was strange he'd brought up the subject when their truce was still at a delicate stage. It was almost as if he was giving her an opportunity to discuss the pregnancy, to say the words she'd almost said before—it's your baby.

Her heart quailed at the thought and she regretted not telling him, although all her reasons for keeping it a secret had seemed valid at the time.

'Shall I turn here or are we going somewhere else?'

Angus's question brought her mind back to the job at hand and she indicated that he turn. He swung the car deftly left, towards the underground parking area of the huge Pacific Far shopping centre.

Over breakfast they talked of work, and the patients she'd be passing on to him—anything to keep her mind off the moment of revelation which she knew must surely come before too long.

Then they went into the department store.

Trawling through here and the various baby boutiques in the early part of her pregnancy had convinced her this was as good a place as any, but she was unprepared for the emotional onslaught of seeing Angus holding up a tiny singlet, his hands gentle as if he already held the baby for whom it was intended.

'Surely it's far too small,' he exclaimed.

Jen shook her head, unable to speak, but he must have sensed her mood and moved to put his arm around her.

'Hey, you can do this,' he prompted. 'I'm here to help and together, you and I, we can do anything!'

She smiled through her tears, recalling the times they'd urged each other on with those words—beginning in the years of study when exams had loomed as the ultimate challenge.

'I wasn't teary over the disaster,' she admitted. 'It was seeing you with that singlet in your hands. This pregnancy business has reduced me to a sentimental mush.'

He grinned at her.

'My stomach did a bit of a jitter as well.'

And so it should, she was about to say, the words finally ready to be said, but suddenly a shift within her body warned her something was happening, then moisture told her what.

'I have to go. We've got to get out of here,' she said, grabbing Angus's arm and hurrying him towards the escalators. 'Next floor down and the side exit—that should be closest to the car.'

Angus went with her, his mind cursing silently as he guided her around couples and through groups of people, steering her towards the door.

'Real contractions?' he demanded when they reached the relative privacy of the car park.

'More immediate, I'm afraid,' she said, a funny kind of wonder in her eyes. 'I think my waters just broke.'

They reached the car and as soon as he'd unlocked it she reached into the back seat and pulled out a beach towel they had always kept there.

She folded it neatly and spread it on her seat, then sat down as calmly as if this preliminary sign of labour happened every day.

'Where? What? What happens next?'

He must have sounded like an idiot—looked like one too, standing there beside the door, staring at her as if she was demented.

She smiled and touched his hand.

'Shut the door, get in the car and drive,' she suggested. 'There's no rush so we'll go home. I'll have a shower, check my bag, phone Dick, then, if he suggests it, I'll go to hospital.'

'But we haven't got the singlets,' he protested. 'Or nappies. I made Nellie give them all away.'

This time she laughed at him, although what humour she could see in this situation was beyond him.

'The hospital has heaps of singlets and nappies. They'll dress the baby when it arrives and keep it dressed until it's time to go home. I'll make out a shopping list and Nellie will get what I need.'

'No, she won't,' Angus argued, the words coming out without much forethought. 'Once I'm finished at the hospital—when you've done your bit and delivered her—*I'll* buy the singlets for her.'

He walked around the car and got in, then got out again to search through his pockets for the keys which had mysteriously transported themselves to the wrong pocket. Back inside, he looked at Jen and caught a look of bemusement on her face.

'You're having a pain?'

Panic seized him. He wasn't certain he could handle her suffering.

'No, no pain, but let's go home,' she murmured, then she leaned over and kissed him on the cheek.

Concentrate on driving, he told himself, but he couldn't, too aware of every move she made, every breath she took.

'You're very calm,' he muttered as they pulled up outside the house,

She shook her head, then grinned.

'I'm saving panic for later.'

Yet his anxiety must have transmitted itself to her because when he suggested again that they go to the hospital she didn't argue.

He took her bag and walked her to the car. All the jokes he'd heard, and the movies he'd seen, of dithering expectant fathers were suddenly far less humorous than he'd thought them. Jen seemed so fragile and with the fragility came an increased awareness of how very, very dear she was to him.

'I love you Jen,' he assured her as he tucked her into the car. Then he looked into her eyes, and added, 'Both of you.'

She touched her hand to his cheek but said nothing, then grimaced and he knew the pains were getting stronger. As he drove the familiar route his mind sorted through knowledge. Did too early a loss of the amniotic fluid mean she'd have a more painful labour?

Not that he could mention problems to her. No, right now she needed support. He took his eyes off the road long enough to glance her way.

'You OK?' he asked, and saw her nod.

Then she put her hand on his knee and said, 'I'm glad you're here.'

So am I, he should have said, but right now his overwhelming desire was to be anywhere but here, doubts about how he was going to handle this situation scoring through his mind like the sharp tines of a plough.

He pretended to be adult, composed and sensible, helping her out of the car, carefully refraining from yelling for doctors, nurses, wheelchairs, orderlies.

Into the main reception area where a smiling beauty invited them to fill in forms.

'She's in labour,' he protested loudly—not quite as adult now.

Jen touched his arm to silence him and said, 'We've time to get me properly admitted.'

He grabbed the papers from her, then found he couldn't read them, the words blurring in front of his eyes as a new and dreadful hurdle filled his mind.

'You can sit down in that small room. Take your time,' the receptionist suggested, and he bustled Jen across the foyer.

'I'm going to marry you again, you know,' he said belligerently. 'Just as soon as we can arrange it. So don't put divorced on those forms, put married. That way the baby won't know we weren't exactly married to each other when she was born.'

'The baby won't read hospital admission papers,' Jen objected, spreading the forms on the desk with maddening complacency.

'She might, later on,' Angus argued. 'You never know when kids will get an idea in their heads to check on birth records.'

He fancied Jen was smiling at him, but that didn't mat-

ter. The issue of their marriage was becoming more and
more important to him.

'You didn't say that was OK with you,' he continued.
'Getting married again, not the business about putting it
on the forms.'

She looked up at him and this time she did smile.

'Is that a proposal?'

'No! Yes, I suppose it is. We should get married, don't
you think?'

He sounded pathetic, but that was exactly how he felt.
Pathetic. And inadequate. And panicky.

And she hadn't answered.

In fact, she was bent forward over the desk, the forms
crumpled between white-knuckled fingers.

Damn the paperwork!

He stormed back into the lobby.

'I'm afraid your bookwork will have to wait. Right
now we need a wheelchair and someone to take my wife
up to the delivery suites.'

To the woman's credit, she responded well, summon-
ing, as if by magic, both wheelchair and an orderly to
push it.

Jenessa had straightened up but her face was white,
her breathing rapid. Between them they manoeuvred her
into the wheelchair and minutes later she was settled in
a beautifully furnished delivery suite.

'Doctor will be here shortly,' the nurse assigned to
Jenessa assured her. 'You've a fair way to go so, once
he's been to see you, if you want to walk around, take a
bath or shower, feel free.'

She turned to Angus.

'I'll be in and out of the room, checking on your wife,
at this stage every half-hour, but buzz me if you
need me.'

She showed him where the call button was concealed behind draperies, and when she left he prowled around the room, realising how much medical equipment was also concealed. Although the room had the appearance of a first-class hotel suite, in actual fact it was fitted up for any emergency.

'Do you remember what it's all for?' Jenessa asked, lying back against the pillows and watching his edgy pacing.

'Most of it, but I hope I don't have to use it. Obstetrics was always my least favourite subject.'

'Do you think that's why—?' she began, then doubled over again, clutching at the pillows as if they might hold her back from the edge of some unseen precipice.

Angus rushed to her side.

'Where's Dick? He should be here. What do you have to do? Why don't you have an epidural right now and be done with it? What's the breathing pattern? Oh, hell, we've forgotten Stick!'

Jenessa heard the wail of despair penetrating her pain. When it passed, she was able to answer.

'He's in school,' she pointed out. 'And, as the nurse said, I've got ages to go yet. That was the first real contraction since we were in Reception. That's what, twenty minutes?'

Angus frowned at her, as if unable to understand the language she was speaking, then he straightened up and said, 'You're right. There's a while yet. I'll go and get him. What school?'

He's either gone mad or he wants to get out of here, Jen thought, but she answered anyway.

'Palm Beach–Currumbin High, but you can't go there and drag him out.'

'I won't,' Angus assured her. 'I'll do it properly. See

the headmaster and get permission.' He grinned at her. 'Then I'll drag him out, or at least give him the choice. The kid's been with you all through this, Jen. He deserves to be here for the grand finale.'

The words, and the concern Angus showed for Jason, made her want to cry again and she swiped at the tears.

'Talk about waters breaking,' she joked feebly. 'They're flooding out all over!'

'That's OK,' Angus assured her, as he bent to kiss her cheek. 'I'll tell the nurse I'm going. And you call her if you want to walk or take a bath. This isn't a time for asserting your independence.'

She watched the door close behind him and shook her head. Although, when she considered it, this mad dash to get Jason out of school wasn't any more surprising than some of the other things he'd said this morning.

Had he meant it about getting married again? And would he be concerned about what the marital status on their hospital admission forms if he wasn't committed to them being a family?

She was still considering these questions, and replaying bits of his conversation in her head, when he returned with Jason.

'You don't have to stay,' she told her young friend, but, although he looked as apprehensive as Angus, she knew he'd stick it out.

The phrasing of her thoughts made her smile.

'Now you're here, the two of you can entertain me. Tell Angus how you got your nickname.'

'Shouldn't we be doing something else?' Jason demanded, settling on one side of the big bed and looking anxiously at her.

'Not yet,' she assured him. 'Just keep talking, even if

I double up in pain and make wild faces and strange moaning noises.'

'How did you get your name? It's not as if you're skinny. And why's Jenessa the only one who calls you Jason?' Angus asked, and, as the next contraction began, Jen threw him a grateful look. Listening to them, it would take her mind off what was happening to her body.

'It was a counsellor,' Stick began. 'He helped me get my head together after I'd gone wild. Told me I had to stick to my decision to go straight and that, in case I needed a reminder, I should call myself Stick.'

'And?' Angus prompted, his voice strained as he tried to keep the distraction going for Jen although, the way she was gripping his hand, he must know what she was feeling.

'Jenessa refused to call me Stick,' Jason replied. 'She reckoned I'd done enough to deserve to go back to my own name, but I kept the nickname anyway. Gives you a bit of street cred at school, if you've got a nickname.'

The spasm passed, the pain fading, and Jen expelled the pent-up air.

'You breathing properly?' Jason asked, and Jen realised he'd been every bit as aware of what had been happening as Angus had, telling his tale to humour her.

'I am,' she replied, 'but breathing exercises in classes and breathing exercises here are two very different things.'

Jason must have heard the petulance in her voice and, eyeing her anxiously, suggested, 'Perhaps you should walk. Didn't they say walking hurried things along?'

'You can walk but I'm staying right here,' Jen told him, shifting her position so she could press her hand against her aching back.

'Here, let me rub it,' Angus offered, and she relaxed

against his kneading fingers, a sense of well-being steal-
ing over her with the relief.

'You can talk more,' she told Jason, accepting a glass
of iced water he'd poured for her. 'In fact, that's what
I'd like. More talk.'

'What about baby names?' he said eagerly. 'I know
you said you'd think of that later, but isn't this later?'

'You haven't thought of baby names?' Angus's incre-
dulity stopped his fingers for a moment and she had to
tap him on the arm to remind him of his job.

'I've thought of some,' she said, defensive in the face
of his surprise. 'What did we think of, Jason?'

'Well, you liked Alistair and I liked Tom but that's
about as far as we got.'

'I like Tom,' Angus agreed. 'It's short and to the point,
but not too classy for a girl, do you think?'

'It's going to be a boy!' Jason argued.

'Nonsense, it's a girl, with dark eyes and black hair,
just like her mother.'

As Jenessa listened to them argue she realised they'd
talked of this before. Surely that meant Angus was as
accepting of this child as he had seemed this morning.

And didn't that mean she should tell him the truth?

The thought coincided with a new wave of pain and
she moved away from Angus's hand, needing to bend
forward to cope with it, breathing deeply, in and out,
aware that Jason was breathing with her and that the argument which still continued was being staged for her
benefit now, an effort by her supporters to distract her
from the pain.

'I said talk, not argue,' she told them when she could
speak again.

'It's not that easy when we see what you're going
through,' Angus grumbled. 'Anyway, the only way we'll

solve the argument is by you delivering the child so we know for sure if it's a girl or a boy.'

'I'm doing my best,' Jen told him. 'And if it is a girl, as you're claiming, what name would you choose?'

'Me choose?'

He looked so startled she chuckled.

'Well, it *is* your baby,' she said softly, taking his hand and drawing him closer to her. 'Yours by adoption, if that proposal you made earlier was genuine, and yours genetically, you stupid man.'

He met her eyes and looked deeply into them for a moment, his brow furrowed as if, once again, the language was hard to understand.

'I'm out of here while you two sort this out,' Jason said uncertainly, but Jen grabbed his hand and drew him back into the chair beside the bed.

'No, Jason, you already know the story. You can back me up if this idiot argues with me.'

She turned to Angus in time to see the wonder dawning on his face.

'The night before I left Australia? That was the one-night stand?'

She heard the disbelief in his voice. 'Do you really believe I could have gone from you to someone else? Particularly after that night?'

'But what about the hamster?'

The words were harsh with what she prayed was hope!

'We always knew the hamster test could have been a one-off thing. That you could have had a virus at the time it was done.'

He put his hand on her stomach and she felt a shudder of reaction ripple through his fingers.

'It didn't matter to me,' he said huskily. 'I'd already decided that, you know.'

'Now I'm out of here,' Jason said, but before he could escape Dick Hollingsworth came in.

He greeted Jason with a handshake. 'Good on you, mate,' he said cheerily. 'I knew you'd come through for her.'

Then he looked across the bed at Angus and shook his head.

'You I wondered about, but I'd heard a rumour you'd returned. I'm glad.'

He put out his hand again and Jen watched as Angus gripped it. She could guess what was going through his head, that this child could be conceived by accident after all the effort Dick and other doctors had put in to getting her pregnant.

'I'm kind of pleased myself,' Angus said, then he squeezed Jenessa's hand, that touch and the wonder in his eyes telling her so much more than words could ever reveal.

'Well, now that's sorted out, how about you two support players slip downstairs for a snack while I check out the patient? The nurse tells me she's in no hurry to have this baby so you guys are going to have to pace yourselves.'

'That's a kind way of saying we're not wanted here for the next little while,' Angus told Jason. He bent and planted a quick kiss on Jenessa's cheek, and Jason followed suit, then the pair left the room.

'How long will it take?' Jason asked Angus as soon as they reached the corridor.

It took him a moment to register the question—and then make sense of it. His stomach was still somersaulting about as his mind tried to accept Jenessa's news. Her sudden declaration had jolted him so badly he couldn't separate the emotions into label-able entities like disbelief, anger, relief and, yes, definitely, joy. They were all there, he was certain, but no one dominated for long enough for him to grasp it and examine it—to use his intellect on it and sort out if it was valid or not.

What had Stick asked?

Duration of labour. He pictured a textbook he'd once had and recalled the graph.

'Anything up to eighteen hours in a normal labour. I'm not certain, but I think Jen was having niggling pains all night, which means a lot of the early stuff is already over. The last time the nurse checked she was four centimetres dilated and, if I remember my obstetrics correctly, that gives her about another two or three hours to full dilation and then about an hour before the baby's delivered, but everything's relative—some women go longer, others a much shorter time.'

They walked towards the lift as he explained, one level of his brain delivering the information, another battling to come to terms with this new version of impending fatherhood.

'But the contractions get closer and closer,' Stick protested, drawing him back to the mechanics of what lay ahead. 'And if she's already feeling so much pain with each of them, that's going to get worse and worse for her.'

'She can opt for pain relief if she wants it, like an epidural anaesthetic. The doctor will control the pain however she wants it handled.'

'He can't do anything unless she asks?' Stick's horror at this situation was evident in his voice. 'You know Jenessa. She won't ask for pain relief!'

Angus chuckled.

'Don't be too sure. During my rare terms in obstetrics I heard dozens of women, who'd wanted to do it naturally, opt for pain relief. It's not so unnatural, anyway, and what's on offer these days doesn't take anything away from the miracle of the birth.'

Miracle of the birth! The words sounded in his head. Yes, this birth was a miracle. His and Jenessa's miracle.

The lift arrived and they stepped inside, but even as they were whisked downwards he knew he had to return to the room, to rush back up and tell Jenessa so many things he should have said before, to reassure her of his love and promise commitment to her dream of family.

He dug in his pocket for money and thrust a twenty-dollar note at Stick.

'Order me a cup of coffee and a packet of sandwiches to go,' he said. 'Cafeteria's on the ground floor. I'll get off here and go back up.'

The lift stopped and he stepped out, pressing the button to call another which would take him up again.

Jenessa was alone in the room as he entered, and although she smiled he could see it took an effort.

'It didn't matter,' he said, 'whose child it was. I mean, I'm glad it's mine, but I'd already decided your "two for the price of one" offer was the best I'd ever heard—far more than I had any right to expect. I love you Jenessa, and I promise you my love will grow as exponentially as yours from this day onwards, OK?'

Her smiled widened, then she shook her head.

'Hold onto that thought,' she told him, 'because right now I'm passing into that dreadful stage of labour where all my pain is going to be your fault and I'm probably going to yell and scream abuse at you for getting me into this state.'

He sat on the edge of the bed and took her in his arms.

'Yell away,' he offered. 'If anyone deserves to be called a few names and told a few home truths, it's me.'

She snuggled up against him, then raised her head.

'Did you lose Jason?'

'Stick? No way! He's getting food for both of us. I guess he understood I needed to be alone with you for a while. He's that kind of kid.'

He held her closer and felt the contraction start. He took her hands so her fingers could grip his—so he could share just a little of her pain.

'Talk to me,' she gasped. 'Keep talking.'

He rubbed her back and talked, telling her how much he loved her, how he hoped their child would have the same qualities of caring as their young neighbour. Told her he used Sid's tools to fix the cot and rocker, and how they'd take the baby to see Sid when she was older.

Stick returned and set the food and drinks on a low table by the window, and while Jenessa shut her eyes and rested between contractions they ate. Then, back beside her bed, they talked again, spinning tales to distract her from the pain, stopping only when she signalled she'd had enough, starting again as the contractions ripped through her body.

Two hours later, after a quick but competent check of the patient, the nurse began to open cupboard doors and wheel out equipment they might need, transforming the room from hotel suite to hospital.

Then Dick returned, and Angus knew the end was near. He was no longer thinking like a doctor, his entire being focussed on Jenessa's pain. He sat on one side of the bed, encouraging her with silly words and trite phrases, while Stick told jokes and rubbed her back and talked of things that had happened in his past.

He breathed with her and panted when she was told not to push, stoically supporting his friend although the experience was probably horrifying for him.

Then, as they both watched in total wonder, transfixed by nature's miracle, the head presented, the shoulders turned in Dick's competent hands and suddenly the rest of the body was there, black-haired as Angus had imagined, slippery with blood. The nurse clamped the umbilical cord, then Dick straightened with the tiny wrinkled form wriggling in his hands.

'Here, hold your baby for a moment,' Dick said to Jenessa, then he turned to Angus. 'Remember how to cut the cord?'

Angus glanced across at Stick who was eyeing the newcomer with wonder and delight.

'You want the job?'

Stick shook his head.

'Not me, mate. I'm going to teach him to surf.'

CHAPTER ELEVEN

ANGUS was buttoning his cuffs when a faint cry from the spare bedroom alerted him to other duties. He headed first for the kitchen where he grabbed a prepared baby's bottle from the refrigerator and set it in a jug of hot water to heat.

'It's OK, mate,' he assured the squawling infant as he bent over the bassinet and lifted his son into his arms. 'Dad's here to rescue you, and although I may not smell like your mother, I have the genuine article in the way of specially expressed breast milk ready for your feed.'

As he set the baby on the change table, the dark blue eyes searched briefly then focussed on him. A smile of such delight lit the little face Angus felt his heart turn over. No one had told him he'd feel this way about the small scrap of humanity he and Jen had produced.

He'd thought more of duty than love, pictured 'fatherhood' as another career, important, of course, but hardly all-consuming. If anything, he'd thought Jen would be the one to spoil and cosset the child she'd wanted so badly, yet it was she who'd hold him back, assuring him it was natural for babies to grizzle a little and bad for them to think they'd be picked up at the first complaining cry.

Yet those noises plucked at his heartstrings and played on his emotions in a way he'd never imagined possible.

Not that he loved Jen the less—in fact, if anything, they had never been closer, united by their love for each other, and their devotion to their son. Which reminded him...

'Now you can stop that smiling and gurgling business and listen to me, young Alistair Jason Angus McLeod,' he said, deftly removing the wet nappy and cleaning his son's nether regions. 'Today is a big day for your parents and we're going to need a little co-operation from you in the way of good behaviour to make it perfect.'

He whipped the folded square into position and pinned it with an ease acquired in many such changes, then fitted the little legs back into the towelling suit.

'All done,' he said, draping a dry nappy across his shoulder before lifting his son into his arms and pressing a kiss onto the downy head.

'For starters,' he continued his lecture, 'you're stuck with me for this feed because your mother, bless her romantic heart, is next door, getting dressed. Then Nellie and Carole can fight over who holds you during the ceremony, and later your mate Stick will be in charge here while I take your mother to dinner at the Sheraton. It's become a kind of tradition for the big moments in our lives, although tonight, thanks to certain obligations we feel towards yourself, we won't be staying over.'

He walked into the kitchen, lifted the bottle from the hot water and, in time-honoured tradition, tested the warmth of the milk by squirting a little against his forearm. Satisfied with its temperature, he carried bottle and baby over to the couch.

'You were conceived at the Sheraton, you know, exactly a year ago today,' he added conversationally. 'I'll tell you all about it when you're a bit older. Well, maybe not about the actual conceiving stuff, but what had happened in our lives back then.'

Settling Alistair on his arm, Angus offered the bottle

and smiled as the baby nuzzled at the teat, then, recognising the familiar taste in a different packaging, began to suck noisily.

Jack and Nellie arrived as Alistair finished his afternoon snack, Nellie swooping on him with delighted cries.

'You finish getting dressed—I'll burp him,' she told Angus.

'Remember what I said about behaving,' he said to Alistair, before reluctantly handing him to Nellie.

If anything was wrong with this 'family' business, he decided as he walked obediently towards the bedroom, it was not having unlimited time to play with his son. Although later, when Jenessa had stopped breast-feeding, they planned for her to return to work part time, the two of them sharing the one position at the practice as well as sharing the parenting of Alistair.

When he went to school…

Angus dragged his thoughts out of the future and hunted around the room for the new tie Stick had bought for him for today's celebration. From a distance it looked like a conventionally patterned piece of silk, but up close the pattern was made of tiny entwining hearts, overprinted again and again like a constant affirmation of the power of love.

He found it where he'd left it hanging over the door of the wardrobe, and when his fingers fumbled on the knot he realised he was nervous. Far more nervous than he'd been the first time—almost as bad as he'd been at the hospital. His mind flashed back to the scene in the delivery suite, and he remembered watching Jenessa's pain and wanting to take it from her, to suffer it himself rather than stand helplessly by her side, filled with an overwhelming love for the woman who strained and cursed with equal fervour.

He crossed to the bed and picked up her discarded robe, sniffed the familiar smell of it and whispered the words which had become his mantra.

'I love you, Jenessa.'

The nervousness lessened and he felt the tension flow out of his muscles.

'I love you, Jenessa,' he said again, and suddenly the day was brighter—more exciting than frightening—

'All you had to do was put on a tie,' Jack grumbled from outside the door. 'The minister's here looking for someone to marry.'

Angus pressed his lips against the satin of the robe, gave his tie one final twitch, then walked confidently out of the bedroom. He could see the small group of friends they'd invited gathered on the patio. They gave a small cheer as he and Jack joined them, and he heard a few teasing remarks about practice making perfect. The sun played across the ocean, spangling it with diamond-bright lights. It warmed his shoulders through his shirt, adding to his feeling of well-being, of rightness.

Carole and Nellie, as he'd guessed, were arguing amiably over who would hold the baby—Carole claiming proximity but Nellie having the advantage of possession. Angus greeted the minister, a patient of Jenessa's who was now on his list, and took his place in front of him with Jack standing by his side. Then, as he glanced towards the house next door, his nerves returned for there was Jenessa, his lover and his life, moving towards him like an ethereal vision glimpsed only in the most fantastic of dreams.

She was wearing a pale, longish dress that clung to her renewed shapeliness and seemed to froth about her calves. Even from the distance he could see the splash of yellow flowers on it, flowers that matched the ones she'd threaded through her shining hair and carried in a small bouquet in front of her. He'd heard her and Carole arguing about a bouquet and knew she carried them as a concession to Carole who'd insisted flowers were bridal.

And bridal they were!

Jenessa, his bride.

His heart brimmed with love, threatening to explode within his chest, beating faster and faster as she moved closer. She was nervous, too, he realised as he saw the whiteness of her knuckles where her hand clung to her supporter's arm.

Angus took a deep, steadying breath and turned his attention to the supporter, scanning downwards from the top of the freshly shaven head.

Stick had dressed up for his role as Jenessa's witness or 'bridesmaid'. He was wearing a new T-shirt which read, 'Surf's up, I'm out of here,' and clean, neatly pressed jeans. A pair of new joggers completed the outfit, and a smile the size of Christmas more than made up for any lack of sartorial splendour.

As Angus watched him help Jenessa over the low wall of the patio, he understood what Jen had meant about love growing and expanding to include not only the small family unit but all those whose lives touched or brushed against it.

Love wasn't a selfish emotion, but an all-encompassing one, as strong and deep as the ocean beside which they stood.

Jenessa's kind of love!

He reached out and took her hand, drawing her close to his side, gazing into her face as he tried to remember if she had always been this beautiful. Her brown eyes met his, the promise of that love so evident in them his knees went weak, his mouth dried up and his mind went blank.

The minister cleared his throat to snare Angus's attention, then opened the small book he carried and smiled benignly on the gathering.

'We are—'

'No, this isn't right,' Stick said, interrupting the man before he got into full flow and causing a severe inner disturbance in Angus's intestines as he tried to understand what was going on. 'Alistair should be up here with the two of you because what you are is a family, not just man and wife.'

Angus relaxed slightly, and tightened his grip on Jenessa's hand as Stick darted back to Nellie and lifted the baby from her arms, returning to hand him to Angus.

'Jen's got her flowers to hold so you'll have to hold him,' the young man said gruffly, then he nodded his head to the minister. 'You can go ahead now, Rev. We're ready.'

The minister went ahead, and there, beside the wonder of the ocean and the beauty of the beach, they made vows that, this time, Angus knew would last for ever.

And when the man finally reached the magic words, 'You may kiss the bride,' he put an arm around his beautiful Jenessa and drew her close, Alistair between them making the circle complete, a hugs-and-kisses family.

MILLS & BOON®

*M*akes
any time
special

Enjoy a romantic novel from
Mills & Boon®

*P*resents...™   *E*nchanted™   TEMPTATION.

*H*istorical *R*omance™   ⌁**MEDICAL**
ROMANCE

MILLS & BOON®

⚡ MEDICAL
ROMANCE™

A FAMILIAR FEELING by Margaret Barker

Dr Caroline Bennett found working at the Chateau Clinique with Pierre, the boy she'd adored as a child, wasn't easy. It didn't help that his ex-wife was still around.

HEART IN HIDING by Jean Evans

Dr Holly Hunter needed respite, and the remote Scottish village was ideal. Until Callum McLoud turned up accusing her of treating his patients!

HIS MADE-TO-ORDER BRIDE by Jessica Matthews
Bachelor Doctors

Dr J.D. Berkely had a good job in ER, a delightful son Daniel, and a truly good friend in nurse Katie Alexander, so why would he need a wife?

A TIMELY AFFAIR by Helen Shelton

Dr Merrin Ryan sees that widowed Professor Neil McAlister needs nurturing and she falls in love! But Neil is aware that he could damage her career...

Available from 5th November 1999

Available at most branches of WH Smith, Tesco, Martins, Borders, Easons, Volume One/James Thin and most good paperback bookshops

2 FREE

books and a surprise gift!

We would like to take this opportunity to thank you for reading this Mills & Boon® book by offering you the chance to take TWO more specially selected titles from the Medical Romance™ series absolutely FREE! We're also making this offer to introduce you to the benefits of the Reader Service™—

★ FREE home delivery
★ FREE gifts and competitions
★ FREE monthly Newsletter
★ Exclusive Reader Service discounts
★ Books available before they're in the shops

Accepting these FREE books and gift places you under no obligation to buy, you may cancel at any time, even after receiving your free shipment. Simply complete your details below and return the entire page to the address below. *You don't even need a stamp!*

YES! Please send me 2 free Medical Romance books and a surprise gift. I understand that unless you hear from me, I will receive 4 superb new titles every month for just £2.40 each, postage and packing free. I am under no obligation to purchase any books and may cancel my subscription at any time. The free books and gift will be mine to keep in any case.

M9EA

Ms/Mrs/Miss/Mr ....Initials.....................................
                                                                  BLOCK CAPITALS PLEASE

Surname ....

Address ....

....

....Postcode................................

Send this whole page to:
UK: FREEPOST CN81, Croydon, CR9 3WZ
EIRE: PO Box 4546, Kilcock, County Kildare (stamp required)

Offer valid in UK and Eire only and not available to current Reader Service subscribers to this series. We reserve the right to refuse an application and applicants must be aged 18 years or over. Only one application per household. Terms and prices subject to change without notice. Offer expires 30th April 2000. As a result of this application, you may receive further offers from Harlequin Mills & Boon and other carefully selected companies. If you would prefer not to share in this opportunity please write to The Data Manager at the address above.

Mills & Boon is a registered trademark owned by Harlequin Mills & Boon Limited.
Medical Romance is being used as a trademark.

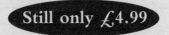